SWIFT ENCHANTMENT

eter Wallis had been Cathy's close
ompanion since childhood and on Peter's
de the affection had grown into an adult
ve. Cathy wished with all her heart that
e could love him in return, but it was
possible. She had given her heart to
n—Peter's friend, although marriage
h Dan was out of the question.
e snatched at marriage with Peter,
realised it would have been better
ver to have married than to live with
love in her heart for another man.

SWIFT ENCHANTMENT

Swift Enchantment

by
Paula Lindsay

Dales Large Print Books
Long Preston, North Yorkshire,
England.

British Library Cataloguing in Publication Data.

Lindsay, Paula
  Swift enchantment.

  A catalogue record for this book is
  available from the British Library

  ISBN 1-85389-984-4 pbk

First published in Great Britain by Wright & Brown
Ltd., 1959

Cover illustration © Pepe by arrangement with Norma
Editorial S.A.

The moral right of the author has been asserted

Published in Large Print 2000 by arrangement with Paula
Lindsay.

Dales Large Print is an imprint of
Library Magna Books Ltd.
Printed and bound in Great Britain by
T.J. International Ltd., Cornwall, PL28 8RW.

CHAPTER 1

The night was warm and a crescent moon looked down upon Buckhurst Hall as though approving the scene. It stood with imposing grandeur on the top of the hill bathed in the moonlight.

A car turned in at the big gates and made its way up the drive. Two men sat in the front of the car, one fair and the other dark. They were welcomed by the sight of fairy lights which had been strung up here and there in the gardens and grounds: music filtered from the big house; young couples with linked hands or arms entwined strolled about the grounds in the moonlit night. Voices and laughter were carried to them on the still air along with the strains of music. A party was in progress at the Hall and it was to this party that the two men were bound.

Peter Wallis stopped the car a little way from the house. Other cars lined the drive. He turned his head and grinned at his companion. 'Here we are!' he announced obviously. 'Better late than never, I suppose.'

'I hope your friends will agree with that sentiment,' was the light reply.

They left the car and strode up to the terrace of the house with its stone steps leading to the main doors. Peter went in with his friend close on his heels. He entered the house with the familiar ease of long custom and hailed their host, Colonel Ames, who was talking to a crony in the hall. The colonel excused himself and came over to welcome them.

'Ha! Peter, my boy! So you finally came—all my girls have been distrait over your absence.' He shook hands with the young man.

Peter introduced his companion. 'My friend, Dan Ritchie.'

'So glad you could come.' The colonel looked about him. 'Make yourselves at home—there's plenty to eat and drink. Excuse me, won't you—I seem to be very much in demand tonight.' He left them and the two men stood for a moment, taking in the scene. An orchestra had been hired for the benefit of the young people and they were seated at the far end of the massive hall with its high ceiling, wide sweeping staircase, open hearth and marble flooring. Several couples were dancing to the music: others sat on the wide staircase, drinking, smoking and chatting; people wandered in and out of the rooms that led from the hall in search of drinks, food or companions.

Colonel Ames was proud of his reputation for being a lavish party-giver and this evening was another of his successes. Very few people had declined the invitation and Peter recognized several of his friends and acquaintances. But his blue eyes anxiously sought only one person in that gathering and his face creased in a smile when he saw her. She was dancing with Major Hardy, a crony of the colonel's, her white skirts billowing, her lovely face turned up to him as he bored her with his heavy compliments. There was no sign of impatience in her expression as she whirled about the hall to his energetic pace.

Peter turned to his friend. 'There's Cathy—the girl I've told you about so many times.'

Dan studied the dancers. 'Which one?' he asked.

'The auburn-haired girl in white. Isn't she lovely?'

Dan followed his gaze as the music stopped and the energetic major released his prey. She excused herself prettily and came towards Peter, for she had noticed his entry with pleasure. She glanced curiously at his companion and their eyes met. She felt a shock of familiarity although he was a stranger to her and for a brief moment she paused in her progress. Only a moment, then she walked on with thudding heart and a mist before her eyes, trembling with a strange, sweet excitement.

Dan felt a surge of uncontrollable longing as he watched her cross the hall towards them. His eyes were on her lovely face and he knew the thrill of enchantment. She was not merely beautiful: there was grace in every movement of her slim, youthful body; her head, held high with unconscious pride, was crowned with a mass of copper curls and a long, curling tress swept over one bare, creamy shoulder. Her gown was white and sparkled with a million brilliants which vied with the diamonds in her hair and at her throat. Dan caught his breath sharply and dropped his lashes as she came near to hide the gleam of wonder in his dark eyes.

She gave both hands to Peter with a warm smile. 'I thought you were never coming,' she accused. 'How late you are, Peter.'

He grinned. He was tall: a fair young

man with an easy smile, a placid countenance and unruffled good humour. His
family owned the adjoining estate, and he
had been Cathy's ardent admirer since she
was a small girl with two copper-coloured
plaits sticking out at the side of her head
and he was a flaxen-haired little boy with
a passion for mischief. They had been
inseparable then for she followed Peter
blindly wherever he led, careless of clothes,
tender skin or state of face and hands.
Returning from an expedition with Peter,
she invariably trotted up to the nursery
with her dress in ribbons, muddy knees
and filthy face and hands, rippling with
childish excitement, full of their escapades
which she would pour into Nanny's ear
while she was hastily popped into a hot
bath and mercilessly scrubbed.

Now Peter replied easily: 'Oh, I knew
you'd go on into the early hours—and I
don't suppose we've missed much.' His
grin widened. 'Anyway, I had to give the
other men a chance before I claimed you

for the rest of the time.' Peter turned to Dan. 'Cathy, I've brought an old college friend of mine with me. He's staying with me—Dan Ritchie. Dan, I've talked enough about Cathy Ames—nothing I said could do her justice. Now you can see for yourself.' Despite the years that had passed since they were inseparable companions on adventurous exploits, Peter still knew that Cathy was the only girl for him. He had loved her long before he reached maturity and Cathy had lost count of the many proposals of marriage he had made. Every time she laughed lightly and told him she was too young to make such a decision yet. It was nearly a year since his last proposal and she feared that another was due very soon. She was reluctant to commit herself although she knew that a marriage between them would please both families.

The dawning flush which Peter's fervent words brought to her cheeks enhanced her loveliness. But she gave Dan her hand and said warmly: 'How nice to meet you at last. Peter used to talk so much about you when he was at college but this is the first time you've been to Chisholm House, isn't it?'

Dan clasped her slim fingers in his strong, brown hand and smiled down at her, showing even white teeth in an attractive, bronzed face. His dark eyes revealed admiration in their depths. 'He used to talk about you too,' he said and his voice was deep and vibrant. 'To tell the truth, I used to tire of the subject, but that was because I'd never met you. Now I understand his enthusiasm.'

Cathy smiled and thanked him prettily for the compliment. Then Peter took her hand and led her away to dance, leaving Dan to stand alone by the marble pillar. She looked back at him and they exchanged smiles. He was such a striking figure. Cathy studied him covertly while she danced in Peter's arms, his fair head very close to her auburn hair. She approved Dan's height, the broad shoulders, narrow waist and slim hips, the pose of his dark head. He was dark enough to be an Italian or a Spaniard, she told herself, with the black, glossy hair which no amount of dressing would ever entirely suppress into sleekness. A tiny smile flickered in her eyes at sight of the dark curls which insisted on framing his temples. Black eyes which seemed to penetrate into her very being, eyes which laughed at her behind dark lashes which were thicker and longer than she had ever seen on any other man. The lean brown cheek, the straight, slender nose, the sensitive mouth which was betrayed by a sensual underlip, an arrogant chin with a hint of a cleft ... But good looks alone could not explain away the sudden lift to her heart, the shock of familiarity, the longing to know him—yet all these had taken possession of her when she first met his eyes. She glanced again in his direction as they swirled past him in the dance. He was watching her and their eyes met. She looked away quickly but not before she caught a gleam of amusement in their black depths.

Peter held her very close as they danced to the slow, dreamy tune of a foxtrot. 'What do you think of Dan?' he asked lightly after a few minutes of silence.

Cathy pulled her thoughts up sharply and it occurred to her to wonder if Peter had known her interest in Dan Ritchie. They were so close and knew each other so well that at times a strange telepathy seemed to exist between them.

'Having only met him for about ten seconds, it's too soon to say,' she countered.

'Well, he's staying with me for a few weeks so you'll have plenty of time in which to form an opinion,' he told her.

'He's very handsome,' Cathy said after a moment and it was almost as though she resented the fact.

'Oh, he's a regular snare for the women,' Peter replied easily. 'They all fall for those Spanish good looks.'

Cathy smiled to herself at his words for she knew what lay behind them. Peter was too placid by temperament to show jealousy but he was quick to point out to other men that Cathy was virtually his property. Just as readily did he warn her about any man in whom she took too warm an interest. She did not however doubt what he said for she could believe that Dan Ritchie was attractive to women. His ready smile, the fascinating dark eyes, the bronzed good looks and his easy charm were all things which would appeal to women—and Cathy Ames was no exception. Disregarding a faint sense of disloyalty to Peter, she resolved to know Dan Ritchie better before he left Chisholm House.

She turned the subject to Peter's visit to Dan's home. 'How did you like Norfolk?' she asked.

'Very much. Dan lives with his grand-father, you know—his parents are dead—and he has practical control of the estate. Of course, when the old boy dies, it will all belong to Dan—about thirty miles of good land! He'll be as rich as Croesus, I should think—and there's a wonderful house to go with it.'

'He isn't married?'

'Good lord no! He'd be a fool to tie himself to one woman when dozens of 'em flock to his side at the lift of a finger. No, Dan prefers to be a free-lance and I don't blame him.'

Cathy looked up at him quickly. 'Would you like to have dozens of women flock to your side, Peter?'

His arms tightened about her. 'Don't be silly, darling. I'm not interested in any woman but you.'

'Perhaps you should take an interest, Peter,' she said slowly. 'You decided that you wanted to marry me before you looked around at other women—supposing you changed your mind later on?'

He laughed. 'Nonsense! I love you, Cathy. I won't change my mind. Speaking of us, anyway, darling ...' He looked around, then stopped dancing and drew Cathy towards the main door. 'Let's go outside for a few minutes,' he said abruptly. 'I want to talk to you.'

She hung back reluctantly. 'Peter—if it's another proposal ...'

He stopped and looked down at her. 'I sometimes wonder if you care anything for me, Cathy.' His voice was low and pained.

'Of course I do. I'm very fond of you, Peter—but give me a little while longer. You must give me time to be sure ...'

'You promised to marry me when we were kids,' he reminded her.

She laughed. She could not help it for he was so painfully serious. 'Darling Peter!' she exclaimed. 'It's a long time ago—and we're not kids now.' Compunction smote her when she looked up into his bewildered, hurt face. 'I expect I will marry you one day, Peter,' she said quickly, 'but I don't want to decide just yet.' She leaned up to kiss his cheek. 'At least, you know that

I'm not in love with anyone else, Peter,' she assured him.

He sighed. 'I suppose that's true,' he muttered.

'Of course it is.' She glanced back into the big hall. 'You mustn't leave your friend alone,' she told him. 'Go and supply him with a drink—introduce him to some people. He looks lonely standing by himself and I doubt if he knows anyone here. Norfolk's a long way from Kent.'

His good humour returning swiftly, he touched her cheek briefly with his fingertips then hurried back to Dan. She watched him go then she walked through the large drawing-room and out into the gardens. She was glad of the fresh air on her hot cheeks and in need of a few minutes solitude. She was not the colonel's daughter for nothing and she adored parties—but this one had been more disturbing than most. It was peaceful in the gardens and she found a favourite secluded corner, sitting down on a seat which stood under an old beech tree. The music faded into the background. She sat there for some minutes, her white dress gleaming in the light of the moon, under the starlit sky, her mouth curving in a thoughtful smile. She hoped to still the heavy beating of her heart which had not yet recovered from the unexpected shock of meeting Dan Ritchie. Her slim fingers played with the long tress which lay over her shoulder.

She visualized the curve of his brown cheek, the laughter gleaming in his dark eyes, the wilful curls which escaped to caress his brow. She could see him so clearly that it was almost as though he stood beside her and the force of her emotions startled her. She longed for his presence, Peter had never disturbed her in such a way. Was this love? Had she fallen in love at first sight with Dan Ritchie?

It seemed incredible but Cathy knew that sometimes love came in so strange a way. Because she was a romantic and a dreamer, she had hoped it would happen to her, one day. Was this the day? Was Dan the ideal she had created in her thoughts who would come suddenly to steal her heart, to bind her round with the silken ribbons of swift enchantment?

She had paid little attention to Peter's remarks on Dan's power over women but now she remembered them with a slight pang. If he made conquests so easily, was it likely that he would take notice of her? If he did, would it be nothing but a light flirtation which he would remember with amusement in later days? She clasped her hands together in swift fear. She could not bear that! This emotion he had aroused in her was sincere and very real although she could not give it a name. The thought that no responsive spark might burn in Dan's breast grieved her and she bent her head while tears sparkled in her eyes as bright as the diamonds she wore.

She was suddenly conscious that she was no longer alone and she looked up quickly to see Dan standing beside her, a quizzical gleam in his eyes. 'I came to look for you,' he said simply in explanation of his presence.

'This is a favourite spot of mine,' she said quickly. 'So peaceful.'

He nodded. There was a stillness in the air and Cathy trembled slightly. He took her hands and drew her to her feet. 'I wanted to dance with you,' he said. The music reached them faintly. He smiled down at her. 'You look like an elf in the moonlight,' he said. 'Ethereal and lovely—but too mischievous to be a fairy.'

'Mischievous?' she queried quickly.

'Yes. What else with that colour hair and the green in your eyes.' He bent his head to look more closely. 'Yes, they are green—I thought so.'

She said, and her voice faltered, 'Shall we go in? You said you wanted to dance ...'

He put his head on one side engagingly and looked at her, his eyes laughing, his mouth curved in a smile. 'Are you afraid of me?'

'No, of course not!' she disclaimed sharply.

'Then don't run away.' There was a note of pleading in his voice now. He lifted the long tress of auburn hair with his hand and the shining, silken curl clung to his fingers as though bewitched. 'Cathryn, you're a very beautiful woman,' he said suddenly. She looked up at him in startled wonder at the words and her heart leaped with joy as though his voice could touch a sensitive string. 'Do you feel as I do?' he asked, so low she could barely hear the words. 'Something happened between us tonight, Cathryn—and I know you feel it too. I never believed in love at first sight but I can't give it any other name. Cathryn ...' He drew her into his strong, protective embrace and her cheek was against his shoulder in the dark coat. He put a gentle hand under her chin and raised her face. Her heart thudded and the blood raced in her veins. She felt weak and helpless in his passionate embrace. She could sense the repressed passion in the man who held her—a passion which found a response in her own innocent heart. As his lips found hers with a surprising tenderness, she hesitated no more and openly betrayed the warmth of her feelings in her answering kiss. It did not occur to her to question the sincerity of his words. Her wildest dreams were fulfilled. Dan had come into her life and taken her heart, giving his own in return. It had been swift enchantment and Cathy was lost in a world of romantic dreams.

He released her at last and she stood with her back against the tree, head flung back. She gazed up at the black velvet of the sky with its myriad stars—and her eyes held their own bright stars.

Dan drew out a slim gold cigarette case and opened it. He offered the open case to Cathy and she shook her head. Helping himself, he fumbled for his lighter which he flicked into life. The flame illumined his dark, handsome face and, watching him, Cathy felt a thrill of love and longing. She put up a hand to stroke the smooth cheek and he caught her fingers in his own hand and carried them to his lips.

Reluctantly, Cathy said: 'We must go back in, Dan. I shall be missed.'

He smiled. 'Certainly you will! I missed the loveliest woman in the room when you slipped away—so will other men!'

She laughed lightly. 'What an extravagant compliment!'

Cigarette smoke wreathed whitely up and about his dark head. He leaned forward to kiss the tip of her nose. 'I can think of many more, Cathryn—but perhaps we'd better return to the house before Peter comes in search of us.' He took her hand and they walked together across the garden towards the big house with its windows blazing with light.

She turned to him, her eyes puzzled.

'Why do you call me "Cathryn"?' she asked.

He smiled down at her. 'It's your name, isn't it?'

'Yes, of course—but everyone calls me Cathy.'

He squeezed her fingers. 'It's a pretty name. Cathryn.' He said it in a low voice very slowly and she thrilled. 'I want you to remember me as someone different to everyone else—can you understand that?'

She raised shining eyes to his face. She nodded. 'It won't be very difficult,' she said quietly, sincerely. 'I've never met a man like you, Dan.'

CHAPTER 2

As they re-entered the big hall, Peter hurriedly excused himself from friends and walked over to join them.

'Where on earth have you two been?' he asked and his eyes held a glint of suspicion. 'I've been looking for you everywhere, Cathy.'

She felt a surge of resentment against his hint of possessiveness but she merely replied: 'I was in need of fresh air—then Dan came to find me to dance with me.' She turned to Dan. 'Do you still want to dance, Dan?'

'Of course.' She slipped into his arms and they sailed away from Peter who stood looking after them with a bewildered expression. Cathy smiled back at him gaily then she gave herself up to the joy of dancing with Dan. He moved easily and well. She was light in his arms and they danced perfectly together, attracting more than their share of attention for they made a perfect foil for each other, he so dark and handsome, she so lovely with the copper hair and creamy skin.

Much as she longed to spend the rest of the evening with Dan, Cathy had a duty to her father's guests and she circulated among them fairly. She was very much in demand for she was popular with both men and women. She danced with young men she had known all her life: sat on the stairs with girl-friends and their escorts, sipping champagne and talking gaily of the party and of others they had been to; was charming to the older guests who thought her a sweet and likeable girl. In the white dress she stood out from everyone else and the colonel was told by several friends that his lovely daughter was the belle of the ball. He did not argue with them for he was very proud of Cathy. She was his only child by his first wife who had died soon after Cathy's birth and though he tried not to differentiate between her and the other children of his second marriage, she was definitely his favourite.

The party broke up gradually in the early hours of the morning. Just after four o'clock, Peter and Dan came to offer their thanks for the entertainment and to say goodnight to the colonel and Cathy, who stood together by the main door. The colonel's arm was about her slim waist and the family resemblance was very marked for he was still a handsome man, though the auburn hair which she had inherited from him was darker and the temples were distinguished with white. His wife was in the middle of a circle of friends who were also taking their leave.

Cathy showed no trace of tiredness for she abounded with youthful energy. Her smile was as natural and warm as it had been at the start of the party, and her eyes still sparkled merrily.

'Come over and have lunch with us tomorrow,' Peter invited. 'If the weather holds, you can bring your bathing suit and we'll spend a lazy afternoon by the pool.'

She agreed readily, then turned to give her hand to Dan. Peter moved to say goodnight to the colonel and congratulate him on yet another successful party.

Dan held her fingers in a strong clasp. 'It was a wonderful evening,' he said in a low voice. 'Thanks to you, Cathryn.'

She laughed up at him. 'You didn't see much of me,' she reminded him.

'No,' he admitted. 'Everyone wanted to be with you and I can't blame them for that.' He grinned. 'Your sisters are attractive,' he said, 'but they don't hold a candle to you.' He gestured towards Bess and Diana Ames who stood with their mother in a circle of friends.

She smiled and drew her hand away. 'I'll see you at Chisholm House tomorrow.'

He nodded. 'Of course—I'm looking forward to seeing you then.' His dark eyes smiled down at her and a faint flush stained her cheeks at the admiration in their depths. Peter bade her a casual farewell and the two men left, discussing the party as they walked to the car. Dan felt a strange reluctance to speak of Cathy and Peter did not ask for his opinion. He took it for granted that all men thought her beautiful and found her personality warm and attractive.

At last Buckhurst Hall was silent and the lights dimmed. The family gathered in the little room which was Lorna Ames' private sitting-room and they sat up for a while over coffee, relaxing comfortably and discussing the party.

Lorna was some years younger than her husband and a very good-looking woman. Almost as tall as he, she could hunt all day without tiring, enjoyed the same masculine tastes as her husband, and came from a well-known county family. It was possibly the strong contrast between Lorna and the delicate wisp of a woman who had been

Cathy's mother that had first attracted him. Stella had never been a companion to him: he had loved her to distraction and her death had been a great blow; for some time it had never occurred to him to marry again but he had known Lorna Denbigh for many years and they met constantly. Gradually, he had sought her company more and more and when Cathy was two years old he had married her. She loved Cathy as much and as carelessly as she loved her own children for she was not a demonstrative woman. It meant more to her when one of her horses broke a leg out hunting or if one of the dogs fell sick than if the girls weren't well or if her son fell from his horse when hunting. She was considerate and kind but casual and her children preferred it that way.

'Daddy, that's the best party we've ever had!' exclaimed Bess fervently. 'I danced every dance and the Brent boys told me they hadn't realized that I'd grown up so much.' She sighed rapturously. 'Isn't

David Brent nice?' At seventeen she was just maturing from the adolescent stage. She was a débutante and the gay social round was never quite gay enough for her. She loved it all—parties, the lovely clothes, the thought of the court presentation, the garden parties, staying at the London flat while she enjoyed a whirl of social occasions. Lorna had made the effort to launch her eldest daughter although the whole thing bored her and she would be well-pleased when the season ended.

Bess resembled her mother strongly for both girls took after Lorna in features and colouring. Dark-haired with grey-blue eyes, tall and long-legged, attractive, their voices possessing the easy drawl they had unconsciously learnt from their mother.

'Well, I'm glad it's all over!' Diana said. 'I warned you I'd tear this dress, Mother—it's too full and flouncy for me.'

'It looked very nice, Diana,' the colonel assured her. 'I was proud of my ugly duckling who turned overnight into a lovely swan.' He rumpled the short dark hair which was cut in a careless urchin style. She grinned at him. She was only sixteen. He thought she should have been his elder son for she had a slight, boyish build, refused to grow her hair, had little patience with clothes and parties and resented the fact that as she grew older she would be presented like her sister and have to be demure and ladylike. Diana loved to wander about the grounds in slacks and sweater, munching apples, talking knowledgably to the grooms about the horses or to the gardeners about plants and pruning. She rode her horse recklessly, swam and fished with her brother, climbed trees with him or tramped for miles over the fields, careless of her appearance, striving for a boyishness which would outshine any boy. Lorna encouraged her in all these things for Diana was a daughter after her own heart and she sometimes lost patience with Bess who was lazy, scanned the fashion magazines feverishly and talked nothing but clothes, cosmetics and social gossip.

The colonel's son and heir had missed the party for he was away at school. But a large photograph of him stood on the table at Lorna's side and this reminded the colonel that he still had to answer a letter from Michael in which he asked for an advance on next term's pocket-money as he was absolutely stony broke, with the rider that he hoped Dad could afford it when the bills for the party had been paid! He was a thin, sensitive lad of fourteen who darkened his unruly auburn hair with dressing in the hope of changing its colour. He hated his school, had never taken any interest in books or learning, and lived only for the day when he was old enough to take over the management of the estate. In this ambition, the colonel encouraged him for he held the view that farming was the only worthwhile career for any man. Guy Ames would take a spade and dig with any of his farm workers: his tractor was his pride and joy; he owned a large herd of Friesian cattle and bred the best pigs in the district. He was never ashamed of the callouses on his hands or the broken fingernails for he was a man of the soil and his family had been gentleman farmers for generations. His skin was tanned by the sun and wind, his muscles were hard and rippled beneath the coloured cotton shirts he wore, and when he worked on the land with his men a stranger would find it difficult to know which was the gaffer and which the labourers.

He sat back comfortably, listening idly to the conversation while his thoughts were of the morrow's work. Lorna mentioned Peter Wallis and he looked up. 'Nice young chap, Ritchie,' he said abruptly. 'I know his grandfather slightly—big estate in Norfolk—fine land. I suppose Ritchie will inherit all that one day?'

'So Peter tells me,' Cathy said.

'Is that the devastating dark man that Peter brought with him?' put in Bess.

'I thought he was really fascinating—he danced with me twice.' She giggled. 'David was quite jealous—or so he said!'

'I think those Brent boys are ridiculous bores,' Diana put in. 'David told me that he preferred to see me in a dress than in jodhpurs—and I know that isn't true for jodhpurs do suit me and this stupid thing doesn't!' She flicked her blue skirts contemptuously.

Bess ignored her sister. She turned to Cathy. 'Is he foreign, Cathy? He looks so dark and handsome—I wondered if he were French or anything?'

'I believe he has foreign blood,' the colonel replied before Cathy could speak. 'I vaguely remember that old Ritchie's son ran off with some heiress—Italian or Spanish, I think.' He turned to his wife. 'Lorna, your brother used to know the Ritchies. Did you ever hear the story?'

Lorna nodded. 'Yes, I did, actually. Gerard used to be quite friendly with Charles Ritchie. It's years ago, of course—I don't remember it very well.'

'Tell me, Mother,' Bess asked eagerly. 'I love hearing about elopements. Did they elope?' She rested her chin on her hand. 'I think I'll elope one day. Would you mind very much, Daddy?'

'I'll put you over my knee if I think there's anything like that brewing, Bess my girl,' he assured her. 'Choose an eligible and respectable young man from a good family—and you won't need to elope!'

Lorna poured fresh coffee for Guy and herself. 'Let me see ... I think Charles went to Spain for material for a book—he was a writer, you know, of sorts. Of course, his father didn't approve of that. I don't think they ever hit it off very well. I was surprised that Gerard should be so friendly with Charles Ritchie for he never hunted or went to the races or played bridge—mooned about reading poems and scribbling in notebooks all the time when he came to stay with us! Anyway, he went to Spain and met this

41

girl—she was the daughter of a count or something, I think. Do they have counts in Spain, Guy?' Without waiting for an answer she went on: 'Her family forbade the marriage and old Broderick Ritchie was furious when Charles wrote to say he wanted to marry this Spanish girl. He threatened to cut him out of his will and Charles told him to go ahead as he'd never cared a damn about the estate or the money. They were married, I believe—not in Spain, though. France or Italy or somewhere like that.' She sipped the hot coffee. 'I never heard any more of them. So Peter's friend is Charles' son, is he? I'm surprised! I wouldn't have thought he could breed such a fine-looking and well-built animal.'

'Mother!' That was Cathy's quick protest.

Lorna laughed, glancing at her indignant face. 'Sorry, my dear—but he does remind me of an animal—so dark and powerful. Just like the new black stallion that

42

Dick Baxter bought from the Crowley stables.' She put down her cup and rose. 'Well, I'm going to bed ...' She bent to kiss Guy's forehead. 'Goodnight, my dear—you're looking well-pleased with yourself. I suppose this party is yet another feather in your cap.'

He smiled. 'I hope so. I think it's likely to be the topic of conversation for a few days in these parts, anyway.'

Cathy went up to her bedroom and stood for some minutes at the open window. The gentle breeze fanned her face and disturbed the soft white drapes. Her room was at the back of the big house and she looked across the lawns, past the swimming pool and the tennis courts, to where in the distance stood the home of Peter Wallis—Chisholm House. But her thoughts were not of Peter. She was remembering Dan Ritchie and her heart was playing strange tricks again ... She was thinking of the day that lay ahead when she would see Dan again and she wondered if she would betray herself so that

43

Peter would know that she had fallen in love with his friend. She could not deceive herself. She loved Dan and told herself he was worthy of her love. She knew little of him but that did not seem to matter. She could hear again his pleasant, vibrant voice, see again his dark handsome face and the passionate black eyes, feel again the powerful strength of his arms and the thudding of his heart against hers. Cathy smiled to herself as she stood by the open window in her white dress. Yes, she would be his Cathryn and she would marry him one day in the not too distant future. There were no doubts in her heart and she knew now that she could never have married Peter when her only feeling for him was one of great affection. Her love for Dan possessed her entire being. They would share a love as great as that his father must have known for the Spanish girl he had married against all opposition.

But there wouldn't be any opposition to their marriage. Her father would surely think Dan an eligible choice for his daughter. A member of the well-known Ritchie family, heir to a large estate in Norfolk, a more than adequate income, handsome and presentable ... She would be the envy of all her friends! Cathryn Ames could think of no better fate than becoming Cathryn Ritchie.

She turned away from the window and unfastened the hooks of her dress as a gentle tap came at her door and Bess entered in her dressing-gown and slippers. Cathy stepped out of the gleaming white folds of her dress, picked it up and threw it across a chair. 'Aren't you in bed yet?' she asked lightly.

'I'm much too excited to sleep,' Bess returned.

Cathy kicked off her white sandals and left them lying in the middle of the room. She moved to the dressing-table and sat down to loosen her long hair. Gently, she drew a brush through the silken strands.

'Did you think my dress was all right?'

Bess asked, smoothing the folds of Cathy's white gown. 'I wish Mother had let me have that scarlet dress I told you about—it was an absolute dream.'

'Too old for you,' Cathy told her shortly.

Bess pouted slightly, spoiling her pretty mouth. 'Too old! My God, Cathy, did you see Jennifer Crowley? Her dress revealed more than it covered and it was terribly sophisticated. I was furious. She is three months younger than I am, anyway.'

Cathy swung round to look at her with a smile. 'Do you want to reveal more than you cover, Bess? I thought your dress was lovely—and I noticed that the plunging neckline didn't bring Jennifer any more partners than usual. You were surrounded by men every time I saw you.'

Bess brightened quickly. 'Yes, I was rather the centre of attraction, don't you think?' There was no trace of conceit in her voice. She was candidly honest and Cathy suppressed a smile. At times she felt strangely mature against these

46

younger half-sisters but she tried not to pull her extra years too much. A little reluctantly but honest as always, Bess added: 'They were all talking about you most of the time. You are lucky to have auburn hair, Cathy—and I wish mine curled like yours, anyway.' She sighed for it was a constant source of irritation that she had not inherited the colonel's colouring and that her dark hair needed frequent attention to keep it pretty and curling. She leaned over Cathy's shoulder and studied herself in the mirror. 'Oh well, I've got little ears and long lashes,' she consoled herself.

Cathy laughed and slapped her bottom with the back of her hairbrush. 'Go to bed, you vain little minx,' she said lightly.

'But I have, haven't I?' insisted Bess, pushing back the dark curls to reveal pretty, shell-like ears and fluttering her long dark lashes violently.

'Yes, you have—and if it makes you any happier, I wish my ears were as small and my lashes as long as yours.'

Bess hugged her and tripped to the door gaily. 'Goodnight, Cathy!' When Cathy thought the door was closing behind her, she put her head in again and said thoughtfully: 'You know, if you decide not to marry Peter Wallis, perhaps I will—he's rather nice, you know.'

'Yes, I know—but perhaps he wouldn't want to marry you,' Cathy said with a laugh.

'When you've made up your mind about him, let me know,' Bess suggested, 'and then I can plan my campaign.' This time the door did close behind her and Cathy put down her hairbrush. Resting her chin on her hands, she looked into the mirror but she did not see the lovely face which looked back at her, the green eyes serious and thoughtful now, the lips slightly parted to reveal small white teeth and the tip of a pink tongue. She had made up her mind about Peter but she realized that he would be hurt by her decision and she was reluctant to tell him. All her life, Peter had been someone important to her. They had shared so many memories and it seemed now that all those childish escapades came back to remind her of their closeness throughout the years. He was almost a part of her and he was certainly an integral part of her life. The future without Peter seemed empty and cold—and yet there was no place for him in her life once she married Dan. She assumed that they would live at his home in Norfolk and it was miles away from Kent. Of course, Peter would still be their friend and they would see him often—but things would never be quite the same again and she knew a nostalgia for their childhood when life was not complicated by love and marriage. They had played together innocently, planning pranks and new adventures, sometimes squabbling, but mostly loyal friends bound by a mutual affection. The affection still existed but on Peter's side it had grown into an adult love and Cathy wished with all her heart during those minutes that she could return his love.

It was impossible now for she had given her heart into Dan's keeping and she had but one regret—that Peter would be hurt. But her love for Dan was something which had suddenly come into her life and she could not help her emotions. Peter would surely understand—he had never failed her yet and it was not her fault that she couldn't love him as he wanted.

The sun was rising when Cathy eventually fell asleep between the cool sheets, her auburn hair falling across the pillows, long lashes curving on her cheeks and an expression of enchantment on her lovely face. The sun peeped in at her window and sent its ray to caress her as she slept.

CHAPTER 3

Laughing, Cathy gave her hand to Dan and he pulled her up out of the blue-tiled swimming pool. She stood on the tiled surround, dripping water, her slimness emphasized by the black swimsuit which clung wetly to her youthful body. Her hair was piled high on her head but a few wet tendrils escaped about the nape of her neck and her brow.

Dan looked down at her and his hand tightened on hers. Sudden longing surged through him and it was revealed in the glance he gave her. Their eyes met and she was very conscious of his closeness. He towered above her, big and powerful and very masculine. His bare chest was as bronzed as his face and his dark hair was wet and curling wildly over his head. His chest heaved from the exertion of racing her down the length of the pool. He was a powerful swimmer, his strokes cutting through the water cleanly and swiftly. It had been an easy victory although Cathy was no mean swimmer herself and her easy, lithe grace had earned his admiration.

Peter lay basking in the sun a few yards from them. Despite his fair hair and skin, he did not burn and he loved the sun. He had refused to swim, assuring them that he was much too lazy for such energetic sport on a hot day.

He watched them through half-closed eyes and he was not blind to the attraction which surged between them. He sat up with a sigh which expressed the fear in his heart and reached for his cigarettes.

Still holding hands, Dan and Cathy came over to join him. Peter threw Cathy a thick towel and offered Dan a cigarette. Dan dropped to the grass beside his friend and took the proffered cigarette with a murmured word of thanks. He ran his hands through his black hair, smoothing back the unruly curls. Cathy towelled herself briskly and then sat down beside them.

'I enjoyed that!' she exclaimed emphatically.

Peter nodded, not trusting himself to speak for the moment. During the last few days, he had seen and understood the signs which meant that he had lost Cathy to his friend. He had accepted the situation but acceptance did not ease the pain. He had been forced to sit back and watch Dan bind Cathy more and more with his personality and charm, his good looks and easy manners, his ready smile and laughing black eyes. He had watched them together and seen the naked love in her face: seen their hands touch and the fingers curve to clasp with eagerness; seen the joy in her eyes when she looked at Dan. He had watched them ride together, racing their horses in competition across the fields and over the low hedges and stone walls. He had looked on while they swam and frolicked in the blue-tinted water of the pool: he had walked beside them while they tramped over the fields with linked hands, laughing and talking together, engrossed in each other, almost forgetting his presence; he had busied himself with choosing records while they danced to the music he provided for them, moving gracefully and in perfect accord, lost in each other's arms, the dance music an excuse to be close in an intimacy in which Peter had no part. With pain in his heart, he had seen the girl he loved giving her youthful love to Dan and he was powerless to prevent this thing which had sprung into life between them. If Dan returned the love which she revealed so obviously, Peter was willing to stand aside and let her find her happiness. But he had seen all this before with Dan and it had been nothing more than an enjoyable game. His Latin temperament and fiery passion sought an outlet and he had loved many women briefly. But Peter could not say any of this to Cathryn while the joy of first love touched her face with radiance, giving her fresh and previously unseen beauty. He could not tear down the veils of illusion and destroy her happiness in Dan. This might after all mean as much to Dan as it did to Cathy, he told himself firmly, and he had no right to interfere. But he dreaded that one day Cathy would be hurt, her love rejected in the casual manner that Dan chose when he had tired of a woman, and Peter knew he could not bear to see the joyous light fade from her eyes and know her youthful, impulsive heart ached for the man she loved.

Cathy did not mean to be thoughtless. She was so lost in the deep waters of first love that she did not realize the effect her response to Dan's charms had on Peter. She barely noticed that he was subdued and a little sad at times for her own happiness brought a gaiety and an excitement which bubbled over and around her. It was important that Dan should enjoy his stay at Chisholm House and she made every effort to ensure his enjoyment.

She turned to him now. 'My father has invited you and Peter to dinner tonight. You will come, won't you?'

He smiled. 'Of course. Convey my thanks to your father.' He exhaled cigarette smoke which wreathed up into the warm air. 'Move into the shade, Cathryn,' he added. 'You'll burn if you're not careful.'

She did so for she had the delicate skin which accompanies auburn hair and already her nose was covered with freckles which she hated but which Dan assured her only enhanced her attractions. 'How brown you are!' she exclaimed, not for the first time. 'I adore tanned skins and you're so dark you tan beautifully.'

He grinned, his white teeth even whiter in the face which had bronzed deeper in the recent hot sun.

'Dan's brown even in the winter,' Peter put in casually. 'It's his foreign blood, I suppose.'

It was the first time his mixed parentage had been mentioned and Cathy seized on the subject eagerly for she was curious to know more about his background.

'Your mother was Spanish, wasn't she?' she asked, playing with a blade of grass.

Dan nodded. 'Yes.'

'Do you remember her? How old were you when she died?'

'Ten.' His answers were curt and it was obvious that he was reluctant to discuss the subject but Cathy did not notice his reluctance.

'Did your grandfather really cut your father off without a penny?'

'Who told you that?' he demanded, frowning. He looked very fierce when he frowned, his dark brows lowering over the darker eyes.

She shrugged. 'I thought everyone knew it. Did he, Dan?'

'I really don't know.' He added: 'He might have threatened it but he didn't have the time to carry it out. He's been very good to me, anyway. When my mother died, he took me into his house and brought me up—he made the long journey to Spain to take me away from my mother's family.'

'Did you mind? Would you rather have stayed in Spain?' she asked.

He shrugged. 'Why not? My mother's family are rich and titled—my life would have been very similar, I expect. I was very happy in Spain—but that's a long time ago.' He turned to Peter. 'Have you heard from Cleo? Is she coming next week?'

Cathy glanced up in surprise from the blade of grass she was splitting with her long finger-nails.

'Yes. She's driving down with Noel on Monday.'

'Good.'

Peter said to Cathy: 'Do you know Cleo Vanney? I can't remember.'

Cathy shook her head. 'No. Who is she?'

'The daughter of the industrial magnate, Sir John Vanney,' Dan provided. 'They live near me in Norfolk. Peter suggested that she should come here for a few days while I'm here then we can go back to Norfolk together.'

A pang of jealousy assailed Cathy and she looked from one to the other of the two men. Peter met her eyes frankly but Dan lay back on the grass, stretching his long body luxuriously in the sun. A smile was flickering about his lips and this did nothing to ease the fear in her heart. She rose to her feet and snatched up her white robe.

'I'm going in to change,' she said abruptly and walked away from them over the lawn towards the house.

Dan sat up quickly. 'Did I say something wrong?'

'Not really,' Peter had to admit. 'But I don't think Cathy's going to like sharing you with Cleo.'

'There's no question of sharing me,' Dan said curtly.

Peter stubbed his cigarette into the soft, warm earth. 'I suppose you know that Cathy's in love with you?' He had not meant to ask the question but it slipped from his lips almost of its own accord.

'Yes, I know.' Dan replied curtly.

'It's none of my business,' Peter said hastily. He had experienced Dan's anger before and he did not want to rouse it now.

'She's a sweet and lovely girl,' Dan said slowly. 'I'm very fond of her.' He glanced defiantly at Peter. 'I may even marry her. I'm sorry, old man—I know you're mad about her, you have been for years, but it's obvious that to her you're nothing more than another brother.'

'All right!' Peter snapped the words sharply. 'And Cleo?'

Dan shrugged. 'So her old man wants me to marry her? I like her—she's a damn attractive woman but I'm not marrying any woman because her father thinks I should. I'm in no hurry to marry at all ...'

'Don't hurt Cathy, that's all I ask!' Peter said sharply.

Dan laid a hand on his friend's shoulder. 'I don't mean to hurt her, Peter. Believe me, no other woman has made me feel like this before ...'

'I've heard it all,' Peter interrupted. 'You said that about Nancy Marsh. I vaguely remember hearing the same thing when you were mad about Paula Heron. I also recall a girl named Vivienne Nash ...'

'Don't go on.' Dan withdrew his hand from Peter's shoulder. 'Okay, so I've loved a few women in my time—hasn't any man? Perhaps I'll meet someone else who can erase Cathryn—perhaps I won't. I don't ask any woman to fall in love with me, Peter.' His voice was low and angry.

'Why don't you try being unpleasant to them?' Peter asked. 'The trouble is, old man—you're not just a pretty face. Women seem to find so many things attractive about you—and don't say sour grapes! I've never wanted any woman but Cathy—and I ought to punch you on the nose for taking her away from me.' He could not be annoyed with Dan and, despite his loss, he laughed lightly, and his voice was teasing. He leaped to his feet. 'Come on, Dan—we'd better change too if we're going into Canterbury to see that film.'

Dan looked up at him. 'You're a great person, Peter,' he said and his voice was very serious. 'I almost wish that Cathryn preferred you to me—you'd make her a good husband and I'm not even sure I want to marry her.'

'Just remember this, Dan ...' Peter paused, biting his lip, then he went on steadily: 'Cathy is different to the other women you've known. She's younger, for one thing, and very romantic. She's fallen in love with you impulsively although she knows scarcely anything about you—I know Cathy and believe me, Dan, she's hearing wedding bells. If you let her down, you'll break her heart—so ease off now while you still can if you're not in love with her.'

Peter turned away and began to collect the towels and cushions. Dan got slowly to his feet. He watched Peter's back in silence for a moment, then he said: 'You're probably right. Perhaps it's a good thing that Cleo is coming next week ... Cathryn will be hurt—but better to hurt her a little now than break her heart later on.' He sighed. 'She is young—so let's hope her feelings will mend quickly.'

'You've made up your mind not to marry her,' Peter accused sharply, swinging round.

Dan shrugged. 'I couldn't settle down— I'm not ready for marriage. I like my freedom and I've not yet met the woman who could compensate for the loss of it. I'm very fond of Cathryn—' He sighed. 'You won't believe me but I do feel differently about her than I ever did about the others. If I thought it would last and if I thought I could make her happy, then I'd ask her to marry me. But I'm a restless devil—and Cathryn's too good for me. She's sweet and innocent and she deserves a better husband than a reformed rake who might be tempted to slip into his old ways!' He clapped Peter on the shoulder. 'As soon as Cleo arrives, I'll do my damndest to show Cathryn that I'm nothing but a fickle and despicable flirt—perhaps she'll quickly realize how silly she was to depend on anything I might have said or done.'

They entered the house together, Peter sober and yet with a flicker of hope that it might prove to be the case, Dan deliberately light-hearted and talkative as though he concealed his ability to feel as deeply as other men. He had spoken truthfully to his friend. He was in love with Cathryn Ames and his emotions went deeper than Peter suspected. But he was troubled by the ten years which separated their ages: the fact that there had been many women in his life but she was innocent and untouched and this was first love which transformed her from a girl to a woman; he had never imagined himself as a marrying man and he was indeed a restless devil, as he had reminded Peter—he loved Cathryn too much to risk making her unhappy in an unsatisfactory marriage. He realized now that he had been wrong to encourage the love which had obviously blossomed at their first meeting but he had been driven by a force he could not control, a greater longing than he had ever known in his life and he had snatched at this chance to know her sweetness and her beauty before their ways parted, as he knew they must.

They had arranged to drive into Canterbury to see a new musical film but Cathy met them in the hall of Chisholm House and said that the sun had given her a slight headache.

'You two go without me,' she said lightly. 'I'll go home and take some aspirin—don't forget that you're both dining with us tonight.'

Dan searched her face anxiously. 'Are you sure? The film isn't important—I'll walk to the Hall with you.'

She shook her head. 'No thanks, Dan.' She turned to Peter. 'While Dan is changing, perhaps I could talk to you.'

He agreed readily and threw open the door of the drawing-room. 'Come in here. It's cool and quiet.' He knotted the cord of his robe more tightly and took her arm. Reluctantly, Dan turned away and ran swiftly up the wide staircase to his room. Cathy followed Peter into the shaded room. He looked down at her and his blue eyes were troubled. 'What's wrong, old girl?'

She came to the point directly. 'Tell me, Peter—that girl you were talking about. Does she mean anything to Dan? Is that why you invited her?'

'I don't know, Cathy. Isn't that a question you should ask Dan? I met her when I was staying at his home—they seem to be on very good terms. She spent quite a lot of time with us. I suggested to Dan that she should come here for a few days and he seemed to think it was a good idea—that's all I know.'

She looked down at her hands, studying the long polished nails intently. 'I was a fool to think that I might be the only girl in his life,' she said, trying to speak lightly. 'After all, you warned me that he had a reputation with women.'

He took her hands and met her gaze levelly. 'I also warned you that he wasn't the marrying type—and he isn't, Cathy. I know you think a lot of him. I'm afraid you're going to be hurt, my dear.'

She looked up at him and there was no disguising the plea in her eyes. 'I love him, Peter. Don't you think he might love me—just a little.'

He nodded. 'I think he does—but not enough to marry you, darling. He likes to be a free-lance—Cathy, listen to me and believe that the fact that I love you has nothing to do with what I say. I've known Dan a long time and he's been in love before—not just once but several times.' He gave a helpless gesture with his hand. 'He's never married though. Doesn't that tell you anything?'

She turned away, releasing her hand from his. 'I understand. You mean he's the kind of man who enjoys being a little in love with every woman who attracts him—I'm just another woman he'll forget as easily as he's forgotten the others.' Her tone was very bitter. 'Thanks for explaining the position to me, Peter. I've been a fool but Dan Ritchie will find that I am very different to other women. He'll remember me when he's left Chisholm House, I promise you.' Her voice was determined now, and Peter frowned.

'What do you mean, Cathy?'

She met his eyes coolly. 'It isn't too late to salvage my heart from the debris of lost hopes and fanciful dreams, my dear Peter.'

He made an impulsive movement towards her. 'Cathy!'

Her hands warded him off quickly. 'No, Peter! Not now.'

'I wish I'd never asked him here,' he said in a strained voice.

'Oh, these things are meant to happen,' she said evenly. 'I expect I'd have met him one day and fallen in love just the same.' She gave a dry little laugh. 'They say that first love is seldom last love—I'll get over it, Peter.' She walked towards the door, her head high and he watched her, admiring the poise which was born of pride and aware again of the courage she possessed, the same courage which had stood her in good stead during their childish exploits and had endeared her to him while other girls had stirred him to contemptuous scorn. She would hide her hurt emotions manfully and proudly and in time would realize that her first experience of love had strengthened her character and endowed her with maturity.

That evening she was very poised and coolly sophisticated, fencing words with Dan in a clever, capable manner over the table, adroitly turning aside his compliments and easy charm, and drawing the colonel's attention to her smooth handling of the conversational gambits.

Dan was puzzled by this new Cathryn yet her brilliant wit and sparkling gaiety drew his reluctant admiration and he realized that there were depths to the girl he loved that he had never plumbed.

She had taken great care over her appearance. A black sheath dress of silk grosgrain emphasized the rich copper of her carefully-dressed hair, the creaminess of throat and arms, the elegant slimness of her slight figure. Emeralds sparkled in her ears and graced the slim throat. Her hands gesticulated often during the conversation that bandied back and forth across the table and the large emerald ring she wore flashed in the candlelight which the colonel affected at his dinner-parties. Her beauty was striking and Dan's eyes rarely left her during the meal. He was barely conscious of the presence of his host or that Lorna Ames on his right was looking very attractive. As far as he was concerned, Cathryn was the only person in the room and this fresh side of her character intrigued and captured him.

After the meal, the ladies withdrew to one of the large drawing-rooms. The colonel sat talking to Dan and Peter over the brandy and cigars for what seemed an endless age to the young men. At last, he pushed back his chair.

'The girls will be expecting us for coffee,' he said. 'I mustn't keep you from them any longer.' He walked beside Dan as they left the room. 'What do you think of Cathy tonight, Ritchie? I've never seen her quite so lovely before.' He chuckled. 'I wonder if all this is in your honour, young man!'

Dan smiled. 'I wouldn't presume to think so, sir. But I agree that she's looking very lovely—you must be very proud of her.'

'I am indeed. And I'm in no hurry to lose her but I suspect that quite a few young men are anxious to take her away from me.' He clapped a hand on Peter's shoulder, turning to him as he followed them across the hall. 'You for one, eh, Peter? When are you going to persuade my girl to marry you?'

'One day, I hope,' he returned lightly and glanced at Dan who raised his dark eyebrows quizzically and shrugged his broad shoulders almost imperceptibly.

CHAPTER 4

Dan followed Cathy out of the drawing-room on to the stone terrace. She turned at the sound of his footsteps and smiled but there was no familiar warmth in her eyes.

He came to stand beside her as she leaned against the stone balustrade. For a few moments there was silence while they both looked over the lawns and gardens. Dusk was just falling and a few stars were already peeping down on the scene. The smoke from Dan's cigarette was carried away by a light breeze which ruffled the flimsy black stole about Cathy's shoulders.

He turned slightly and gazed down at her. She raised her face and met his eyes evenly. 'It's a pleasant evening, don't you think? I shall be sorry when the summer comes to an end.' Her voice was cool and faintly brittle.

He frowned. 'You're very distant tonight, Cathryn—or is it all part of the new sophistication you seem to have acquired?'

A smile flickered about her lips. 'Don't you like it?'

'Not particularly.' He was blunt. 'Maturity doesn't rest prettily on your shoulders, my dear—don't try to be older than you are.'

A faint flush stained her cheeks. It might have been annoyance but she gave a light laugh. Lorna had sat down to the piano in the drawing-room and the music reached them faintly. She put up a hand and began to play with the flimsy folds of her stole.

Dan captured her hand in his. She gave him a slightly amused glance. 'I have a strange feeling that you're angry with me,' he said in a low voice. 'Am I right?'

'Angry? Why, of course not.'

He did not look at her now but her fingers were still clasped firmly by his hand and she made no effort to draw them away.

'I've noticed a distinct coolness in your manner since Peter and I mentioned Cleo Vanney,' he went on. 'Any connection?'

She raised her chin proudly. 'Why should it matter to me that one of your friends is coming to stay at Chisholm House?'

'Because you're jealous?' he asked and he turned to smile at her.

'My dear man, I have no claim on you,' she assured him lightly. 'I'm rather interested in meeting Cleo Vanney.' She threw him a mischievous glance. 'Is she a good example of your taste in women?'

He shrugged. 'Cleo and I happen to live on adjoining estates,' he said slowly. 'We're friends—and that's all.'

'How interesting! Is she attractive?'

'Yes,' he said curtly.

'I hope Peter doesn't succumb to her charms,' she said flippantly. 'I'd be lost without my Old Faithful in the background.'

He bit his lips. 'I suppose your family would be pleased if you married Peter?'

'Of course they would. I think they've visualized it since we were both in rompers.'

'Have you ever thought seriously about marrying him?' he asked abruptly.

She raised her eyebrows. 'Isn't that rather a personal question, Dan? You shouldn't pry into a girl's heart,' she told him lightly.

'I thought I knew your heart,' he said strangely.

For a brief moment she longed to steal into his arms and hold him close, renewing the intimacy they had shared—but pride held her back as she recalled Peter's words and she merely said coolly: 'It's easy to make mistakes.' She moved away from him, withdrawing her hand.

He took a step towards her and the next moment she was in his arms. 'I'm not mistaken!' he said fiercely, and then his lips were searing her slightly-parted mouth. He raised his head and searched her eyes, his own triumphant at her instinctive response.

She recovered herself quickly and looked up at him with laughter in her eyes. 'This is so sudden!' she mocked. Without a word, he released her abruptly and turned away, staring over the gardens while he brought out his case and put a cigarette between his lips. He fought to control the surge of anger and the fierce passion which her nearness had stirred in his blood. Cathy stood leaning against the balustrade, her head a little on one side, watching the tense profile, the quick, impatient inhalation on the cigarette, the sharp stab of smoke which he ejected from his lungs. At last he said angrily: 'Don't play with me, Cathryn!'

She laughed again flippantly. 'This man is dangerous!' she said with that brittle note back in her voice. She gathered her stole more closely about her. 'Shall we go in?'

He followed her back into the drawing-room and watched her sit down on a comfortable settee beside Peter. Dan walked over to the piano and leaned on the top, talking to Lorna who continued to run her fingers idly over the keys, picking out snatches of melody. Bess was sitting on the arm of the colonel's chair, her soft pink dress with its youthful lines enhancing her dark prettiness. Diana had reluctantly changed for dinner but her dark hair had received the minimum brushing and she looked ill at ease in the blue dress she wore. She was flicking idly through the pages of a magazine which Bess had devoured eagerly earlier that day. Diana showed little or no interest in the fashionable styles of clothes and coiffure it portrayed. A few minutes later, she threw it aside and called Dan over. They began a discussion on horses and hunting. There was no sign that he thought of her as a mere child in his concentration on her remarks for she was knowledgeable on this subject at least and, despite her boyishness, possessed an odd maturity which her sister Bess lacked.

Cathy paid little attention to Dan during

the rest of the evening. She was her most charming self to Peter who had observed her display of sophistication with some admiration and a little amusement. He wondered idly at her motives. Did she mean to prove to Dan that she was no youthful innocent who had fallen an easy prey to his undeniable charms? Or did she strive to convey the impression that she was as capable of coquetry and sophistry as he? Peter also wondered, with an oblique glance at his friend who seemed absorbed in his conversation with Diana, what had been Dan's reaction to Cathy's behaviour.

Later, as they walked back to Chisholm House through the grounds of the colonel's estate, Dan turned to him abruptly and said: 'I'd like to know what you and Cathryn talked about this afternoon. I'm sure your conversation has some bearing on her strange aloofness this evening.'

Peter shrugged. 'Our conversation was private, Dan. Sorry—but I don't break confidences.'

'Oh, I can guess!' Dan said curtly. 'No doubt she asked you—as my friend—if my intentions were honourable towards her. And you—also as my friend—pointed out that my intentions have never been honourable yet where a woman is concerned.' Suppressed anger rang in his voice and his eyes glinted dangerously.

'You can't blame me for wanting to protect her from being hurt,' Peter said stonily. 'In case you've forgotten, I happen to love Cathy. I've loved her for years and I'm determined to marry her ...'

'By fair or foul means?' sneered Dan. 'What makes you think she'll marry you?'

'She will,' Peter replied confidently. 'When she realizes that this love she feels for you is nothing but an infatuation.'

Dan stopped short, clenching his fists. 'You really believe that?'

Peter was too basically honest to prevaricate. 'No, I don't,' he said shortly. 'But I intend that Cathy shall think so.' He faced Dan squarely. They were much of a height and blue eyes met black eyes fearlessly. 'Look here, Dan, I've no quarrel with you.'

'I'm not trying to quarrel,' Dan said soberly. 'I can understand the way you feel, old man—and I agree with you in most of the things you've said. I know that Cathryn's happiness is your only consideration.' He sighed. 'I also know that she'll be a damn sight happier as your wife than mine. So I'm prepared to do whatever you say and leave you a clear field.' It cost him an effort to say this but he had made the decision earlier and he would not swerve from it now.

They walked on. 'Cleo will be here soon,' Peter said slowly. 'Turn your charms on her and Cathy will soon realize that she doesn't stand a chance with you. There won't be any embarrassing scenes—she's too proud for that!' He cast a sideways glance at Dan's profile, noting the lowered brows, the grimness of her lips, the tiny nerve which jumped in his cheek. 'I'm not asking much of you, after all,' he went on impatiently. 'You obviously don't care enough about Cathy to consider marrying her but I do. I've never wanted any woman but Cathy—good lord, man, you know that! Leave her to me—pretend you've tired of her or that Cleo means more to you!' He laughed dryly. 'I shouldn't have to tell you how to rid yourself of a doting girl-friend!' He paused and searched Dan's face anxiously. 'Well, Dan?'

The answer was a shrug of the broad shoulders. Dan's thoughts were in turmoil. Dan had convinced himself that he was not the man to make Cathryn happy so it was surely better to let her think that he was nothing more than a careless flirt who had appreciated the opportunity of a fresh conquest. Cleo was the obvious and available cover for his real emotions. She would appreciate his attentions for they had shared a mild affair in the past and Dan knew that flirtation was a mere game to her. Grimly, he told himself that Cathryn would turn to Peter for comfort and would find his loyal and loving friendship a better and worthwhile thing than the fickle attentions that Dan had offered her. There was a determination in Peter's character which Dan had met before and he knew that his friend could probably bring gentle and subtle persuasion to his suit so that in time Cathryn would agree to marry him. Peter would make a good husband, Dan thought with a wry twist to his lips. He had all the assets which Dan lacked: loyalty, unshakable good humour, stability and reliability, a certain acceptance by her family and friends. The only things Dan could offer her was an ardent love and a marriage of fire and fury which might eventually fade into cold ashes. Dan did not deceive himself. He knew his own failings—yet there was a conviction deep in his heart that this time love was binding, all-embracing and strangely unselfish. Life could deal cruel blows but his main concern now was for Cathryn and he wished there were some way he could keep her from the painful knowledge that she had fallen in love with a rake. Although he had assured Peter that she would probably soon get over it, there was no such certainty in his private thoughts. The flame which had leaped into life with such startling and sudden brilliance was not one which would be easily quenched. With a rare insight, he realized that swift enchantment had brought lasting bonds and that no matter where circumstances may turn their separate paths, an irrevocable tie would still hold them. It was anguish to contemplate his life without her—yet she would never be happy sharing the life he led. He doubted if he could be truly faithful to any woman, even to Cathryn, for his Latin blood had endowed him with fierce passions and a disregard for conventions. Rather than make a mockery of the marriage vows, he had decided never to marry. Until now, he had never met any woman he wanted for a wife. His quick temper, too, was a fault which would mar any marriage. His blood ran hot with anger at mere trifles and his tongue flashed with venom without forethought. He had strange moods and sometimes left the Norfolk house without a word of warning, staying away for days or weeks, returning without explanation. Only he knew that on these expeditions he roamed the countryside for miles, sleeping rough or camping with gipsies, accompanied only by his faithful dog, possessed by a strange desire to be free from all ties and conventions. Was this the kind of life he could ask any woman to share? Least of all, a young girl like Cathryn who had grown up in a happy and sheltered home, who knew little of the outside world, who still had dreams in her eyes and wore the veils of illusion. Nothing would induce him to destroy her dreams, to tear down the veil of innocence. He dreaded her contempt, her coldness and her lack of understanding.

Peter respected his need of silence and

they exchanged no further remarks until they entered Chisholm House. The butler was dimming the lights and tidying the drawing-room and he wished them a respectful goodnight.

Outside his bedroom door, Dan turned and held out his hand to Peter. 'You're the best man,' he said, 'and I'm retiring from the contest. All I ask is that you make Cathryn happy.'

Peter clasped his hand firmly. 'She'll be happy.'

Dan looked at him. 'I believe she will,' he said slowly and withdrew his hand. The door closed behind him and Peter stood looking at the wooden panels for a few moments. Then he walked along to his own room, his eyes thoughtful, his brow creased in a light frown. His usually placid face was disturbed. He unclipped his bow tie and placed it on a table, his lips pursed in a soundless whistle. He had the odd conviction that for the first time in his life that Dan was deeply affected by a woman he barely knew. Peter ran his hands through his flaxen hair and his eyes were thoughtful. 'A pretty kettle of fish,' he said aloud, ruefully. 'I know Cathy loves Dan—and it wouldn't surprise me if he really cares for her.' He shook his head and addressed his reflection in the mirror. 'But it won't do. I can't let him marry her, old man,' he said slowly. 'I know them both—and oil and water won't mix. Dan's too tempestuous and Cathy's too generous. It might be give and take—but Cathy would do all the giving and Dan all the taking. She'll be far happier with me when she gets used to the idea.' With this philosophical assurance, he turned away from his reflection and began to undress.

Dan lay wakeful for a long time but finally he slept restlessly, his night disturbed by dreams. He had promised to ride with Diana at the early hour of half past six and he reluctantly stirred in his bed at the first rays of the morning sun. He glanced at his watch and threw back the covers.

Diana was waiting for him, impatiently, the grey horse under her almost as impatient for his gallop and fretting at the bridle.

'You're late!' Diana accused as he rode up to join her. 'Trust a man to love his bed in the early morning.' She leaned forward and patted the neck of her mount. 'All right, Beau,' she soothed.

Dan grinned at her from the saddle of the big stallion he had borrowed from the Wallis stables. A cool breeze billowed the white shirt he wore open at the throat. A silk cravat was knotted about his neck and he looked this morning even more like the big black animal Lorna Ames had called him, dark and powerful. Diana appraised him for a moment then she spurred Beau and led the way across the fields, giving her horse his head. Dan was close behind her. The air was fresh and crisp and Diana's short hair flew in the wind as they galloped furiously over field and stream. Dan could not help but admire her capable handling of the big horse, her fearlessness in the saddle, and he noted her ease and self-possession which many an older woman would envy.

They had an early breakfast at a small farmhouse some six miles from Buckhurst Hall. The farmer's wife knew Diana well for she often gave the hungry, windblown girl breakfast after an early ride. Bacon and eggs sizzled on the stove and its appetizing aroma wafted out to Dan and Diana as they sat on the stone wall in the yard, kicking their heels and talking eagerly of their ride. The horses were grazing in a nearby field, their girths loosened, glad of the respite, for they were both hard riders.

Hot rolls, newly baked, and farmhouse butter accompanied the bacon and eggs and they drank strong, hot tea with healthy thirst. They ate a hearty breakfast while they talked of horses, dogs and land.

'One day you must come to Norfolk,' Dan invited. 'I'd show you some land—and

I've some splendid horses.' Replete, he sat with a cigarette between strong, brown fingers, smiling across the table at the young girl.

'I bet you haven't a horse to compare with Beau,' she responded stoutly.

He grinned. 'I doubt if he'd stand up to the hunting we have in Norfolk, Diana.'

She made an indignant protest which brought a gleam of amusement to his eyes. Then she added, glancing at him through dark lashes: 'May I really come to stay with you, Dan? You've talked so much about your estate that I'd love to see it.'

'Not my estate,' he corrected. 'My grandfather owns it, you know. It will be mine one day, though.' His eyes lit up with pride.

'You have the same look that Michael has when he talks of the land,' she commented. 'He wants to go to an agricultural college but my father is set on sending him to Cambridge.'

90

Dan rose to his feet. 'I suppose we should turn back now,' he said reluctantly. 'Peter and I are supposed to be playing tennis this morning.' They bade Mrs Darby a friendly farewell and Dan pressed a note into her hand, with a word of thanks for the excellent breakfast.

She came to the farmhouse door and watched them as they swung up into the saddles and set off in a steady canter for Buckhurst.

They parted at the same point where they had met earlier that morning and Diana galloped off with a light wave of her hand. Dan, reining in his horse, watched her go and then sat still in the saddle for a few minutes, his face thoughtful. Though she was so young, she was an attractive girl with a warm, gay personality. One day she would make a fine companionable woman with many good qualities. It was an unusual thing to find three girls in one family so different from each other. Bess was typical of girls of her age, newly launched on society, frivolous, pleasure-loving and a trifle empty-headed. He doubted if she would change very much as she grew older. Diana had the maturity of an older woman mingled with a youthful boyishness. The latter would gradually be overlaid with other qualities and yet he felt sure she would retain the elfin character he saw in her eyes and the curve of her mouth. Cathryn—and here he paused for he found it difficult to analyse her character. There was a trace of wilfulness in her nature: a hint of cool arrogance in the lift of her chin; but with this she was warm-hearted and sincere, impulsive and generous with her affections, blessed with an inborn charm which would always attract friendship and admiration. He turned his horse towards Chisholm House and spurred him on ...

CHAPTER 5

Cathy leaned on the low stone wall of the bridge which crossed the tiny stream. The water flowed steadily underneath the bridge on its way to join a river some miles further along. She looked down at the clear water and could see the bright stones and pebbles on the bed. Flotsam scurried along in the current—twigs and bright leaves, drifting flowers, a cigarette packet which some village boy had probably thrown from the bank while wandering along the side of the stream in the cool of the evening, his arm about his sweetheart.

The dogs set up a loud barking and she turned to see the cause of the commotion. Dan strode towards her, leaving the cool shade of the copse and coming out into the bright sunlight. He stopped to rub the dogs' ears, pick up a stick which they eagerly ran for, barking their excitement, and then knelt to tighten his shoe-lace. Cathy waited, her heart thudding unevenly. He straightened up and walked on to join her in the middle of the stone bridge.

'Pleasant spot,' he commented.

She nodded. 'Were you looking for me?' she asked.

'No. Just walking.' He smiled down at her. 'Why are you on your own?'

She shrugged. 'Exercising the dogs.' She turned to call them. 'Bruno! Come here, Rex! Carlo—you bad boy, leave the birds alone!' They loped towards her at the sound of their names but the last-named paused to give one last warning bark at the birds who soared, startled, with a flutter of wings and then settled again on the low branches of a tree. Bruno and Carlo were big Alsatians: Rex a black spaniel with big, floppy ears and brown appealing eyes. Cathy caressed them casually, backing away as Bruno raised on his hind-legs to rest fore-legs on her shoulders. 'Down, Bruno!' she said. 'You'll knock me over, you brute!' She stumbled over Carlo and Dan's hand was at her elbow in a moment to steady her. She laughed her thanks. 'They always manage to get underfoot,' she said. 'Where were you heading for, Dan? The village?'

He shook his head. 'I thought I'd stroll through the copse—then as I neared the stream, I caught sight of a green dress and I wondered if it were you. So I came to find out.' He turned with her and they began to walk back towards the copse, the dogs bounding on ahead.

She kept her eyes on the trees before them. He strode beside her, his long legs adapting themselves to her slower pace. 'Your friends arrive today, don't they?' she asked casually.

'Noel and Cleo? Yes, they do—Peter's taken the car to Canterbury to pick them up.'

'They've made the journey by train?' She glanced at him in surprise.

He grinned. 'Well, you see, Noel has been disqualified from driving for twelve months and Cleo told me on the telephone yesterday that she ran her car into a brick wall during the week. So train it is.'

'She wasn't hurt?'

'Cleo has nine lives, I assure you! She needs to have—the way she drives a car! She nearly killed me a few months ago.' He stopped and parted the dark hair, bending his head to show her the scar of a deep cut. 'It was a nasty gash,' he said, 'but I was lucky to get away with just a cut head.'

'What happened?'

'Cleo drove us into a ditch. We were coming back from a party and I confess we were all a little merry.'

'Was anyone else hurt?' Cathy asked with interest.

'Mostly bruises. Cleo was the unlucky one—she broke three ribs and fractured her wrist. But it doesn't make any difference—she still drives as recklessly as ever.'

Cathy was forming her own private opinion of Cleo Vanney and she was already convinced that she would not like her. She had nothing but contempt for the type of person who drove dangerously, risking not only their own lives but also those of others. She had drawn Peter and Dan to talk of Cleo during the last two days and gradually the picture had been built up in her mind. Wilful, selfish and spoilt, a good time girl by all accounts who spent lavishly and lived richly, she seemed to care nothing for convention or the opinion of anyone, family, friend or neighbours.

As though he read her thoughts, Dan said: 'She's very different to you, Cathryn. I wonder if you'll like her?'

'Peter does so there's no reason why I shouldn't,' she prevaricated smoothly. 'We have very similar tastes, you know.'

He nodded. 'Probably because you grew

up together. I imagine that Peter has influenced your character a great deal.'

'We have very much in common,' she admitted. 'I expect you're right.' They took the path through the copse which would eventually lead them to the gardens of the Hall. She glanced up at him. 'It's strange that you and Peter should be such friends,' she said slowly. 'I would have thought you'd clash on many subjects—you're so different in temperament.'

'Oh, opposites attract, don't they?' He grinned. 'We do clash sometimes—but we've never had a quarrel that lasted any length of time. I'm afraid Peter doesn't always approve of me. I've been a bit of a rake, you know.' He gave a slight shrug of the broad shoulders in the pale blue shirt. 'I work hard—so I feel that I'm entitled to play hard, too.'

She made no reply and he glanced down at her, slim and lovely in the soft green dress, her beautiful hair loose on her shoulders in an auburn cascade which framed the delicate cameo-like face. It was going to be so hard to give her up, harder still to hurt her, but he had pledged his word to Peter and in a very short time he would be deliberately concentrating on Cleo. He was dreading the look of contempt which he felt sure would spring to Cathryn's bright eyes. He and Peter had gradually paved the way by speaking often and admiringly of Cleo Vanney and her wild exploits, blonde beauty and elegance. Dan had tried to impress upon Cathryn that he found many women attractive and had quite a reputation in his set. But still a swift, unexpected glance would catch the unguarded worship in her eyes and he would be a fool if he denied the love which she radiated when they were together. He had tried to be casual with her, making no attempt to kiss her since the evening on the terrace, hoping she would think he was already tiring of her charms. Now, as she walked by his side, he had to fight down the urge to take her into his arms and kiss those sweet lips to passion, taking hungrily the love which her generous heart would gladly offer him.

Suddenly she stopped and turned to him, her face lifted appealingly. 'Dan!' she said. 'Dan—kiss me.'

Casting aside all his good intentions, he drew her into his arms and bent his head. Dark head was very close to auburn and their lips met in a long, satisfying kiss. When he finally raised his head, she sighed and snuggled closer to him, her cheek against her shoulder. His hand touched her hair, his fingers entwining in the silken tresses. She could not see his face but she would not have understood the enigmatic expression or the longing in his eyes.

The impulse had been stronger than pride and Cathy did not regret it. She had longed for his arms, to know again his kiss and his nearness, although she told herself that his strange coolness was her own fault for rebuffing him. She sensed that he was a proud man and would not seek a second rebuff. The first move had to come from her and she could not stand the distance between them any longer. Before Cleo Vanney arrived to spoil their intimacy, she had to know that Dan loved her as she loved him. Now she was content. His arms and lips had surely betrayed the depth of his feelings. Innocent Cathy had never been casually embraced by any man with such passionate ardour so it was not strange that she should assume Dan loved her in return. A triumphant smile flickered about her lips for she no longer feared that Cleo's arrival would make any difference to her happiness.

Dan had almost drowned in the love she so generously gave with her lips. His own feelings had left him shaken, desire pulsing in his blood, but as she stood in the circle of his arms, desire faded and he felt only a great longing to share his life with the girl he loved, a protective warmth and affection, a surge of tenderness. He held her close and he knew that this love he felt for Cathryn Ames was the greatest thing that had ever happened in his life. All other considerations dwindled in comparison. He knew also that his love was unselfish enough to stand back and watch her find happiness with another man. He loved her greatly but he lacked the key to her happiness.

He released her. 'Let's walk on,' he said slowly. She sought his hand and held it firmly in her own small, slender fingers, reluctant to lose the intimacy they had shared in those few moments. 'We'll skirt your house and cut straight across the fields to Chisholm House,' he said, as they left the cool shade of the copse. 'I should think Peter is back by now with Noel and Cleo—I want you to meet them.'

She smiled happily up at him, willing to agree to anything he suggested. 'You haven't told me much about Noel,' she chided him.

'Well, Cleo rather outshines him, I suppose. She has far more character than her brother. He's a nice enough fellow but weak. The kind of man who doesn't leave much impression on people—as you'll soon see for yourself,' he assured her.

Cathy realized the truth of his words as soon as she was introduced to Noel Vanney. He had none of the striking good looks of his sister: where she was tall, he was only of medium height; her elegant slimness only served to emphasize his lanky leanness. Her hair was so blonde as to be almost platinum in colour: he was merely fair and a long lock fell untidily over his brow. The brilliant blue eyes which ran over Cathy with a cool disdain were lovely and startling: Noel's eyes were a light, almost colourless blue which heightened the weakness in his facial appearance. He shook hands with Cathy and his grip lacked the firmness which she had noticed in Cleo's clasp.

They had just arrived at Chisholm House when Dan entered with Cathy. Peter turned quickly to greet them.

'Amazing!' he said. 'The train was actually on time.'

Dan went immediately to Cleo and, taking her hands, bent his head to kiss her cheek. 'Was it an awful journey?' he asked warmly.

She flashed him a brilliant smile. 'Hell! But my own fault for smashing the car, I suppose. The garage people looked so gloomy that I think I'd better buy another car and sell that one for scrap.' Her laugh was vivacious and bright. She studied Cathy with a cool smile flickering about her lips and then Peter drew her forward to introduce her. 'So this is the girl-friend you were always talking about, Peter.' It was as though she dismissed Cathy as being of little importance and Cathy felt a glow of anger, resenting Cleo's coolness. It was apparent that she cared little for the society of other women for she turned back to Dan, linking her hand in his arm. 'You're looking very well, darling—relaxation seems to agree with you. But I'm always telling you that.'

He grinned. 'Your idea of relaxation is that I should never do any work at all but spend my days amusing you, Cleo, my sweet.'

'Can you think of a better occupation?' she asked with a provocative glance. 'I suppose you've been collecting hearts during your short stay here, Dan—that handsome face of yours will get you into serious trouble one day!'

'I'll wait till that day and then worry about it,' he retorted.

She addressed herself to Cathy. 'I hope you've been sensible enough to escape Dan's charms. He's a devil, you know—I think he enjoys capturing the affections of every girl he meets.' She tapped his arm with long, painted finger-nails. 'Never mind, my lad—one day you'll meet your match and it will be your heart that gets broken.'

He laughed. 'Impossible! I may love a little—but never too much!' He laid his hand over Cleo's fingers and squeezed them.

Watching, Cathy felt a stab of pain— both at his words and the little, familiar gesture. She could not believe her ears and eyes after knowing his embrace in the copse. But she quickly assured herself that he spoke lightly and in jest. It was not likely that he would wear his heart on his sleeve so that Cleo Vanney could see it.

She said quietly: 'I'm sure Dan isn't as bad as everyone paints him.'

Cleo looked at her in surprise. Then she said mockingly: 'Sweet innocence! Or has Dan been on his best behaviour for your sake?'

Cathy tightened her lips and knew that her instinct had been right. She thoroughly disliked Cleo Vanney.

Her dislike grew stronger during the next few days. With amazement, she watched while Dan paid the girl marked attention and noted the casual intimacy which existed between them. They were always together—Dan smiling down at her with meaning warmth in his eyes, stretching out a hand to touch her fingers or press her shoulder, laughing at a shared joke or memory, constantly talking of things and people that she knew nothing about.

Cathy bravely joined them for swimming, tennis, picnics and expeditions to the surrounding countryside or neighbouring towns. She went to dinner at Chisholm House: rode with them in the early morning; drank cocktails and danced to the radiogram. Never once did she betray the pain in her heart for she was too proud to give Dan the satisfaction of knowing that she was just one more conquest. But she studied Cleo Vanney carefully. She noticed the brittle selfishness of a spoilt woman, sensed the hard core behind the surface of easy charm, observed the blatant, provocative invitation behind her smiles and glances to which Dan responded without fail. Cathy was scornful of the carefully cultivated air of bored sophistication which Cleo adopted and was horrified by the deliberate rudeness she sometimes showed.

Was Cleo really an example of Dan's taste in women? What could he see in her that Cathy was blind to—did she possess some fascinating qualities which would appeal to Dan?

Her love for the dark, handsome Dan Ritchie was slowly breaking her heart. But she realized now that she had given her love to a worthless man for he made it very clear that although he had enjoyed a mild flirtation with her, it had ended with Cleo's arrival in Kent. He now showed her little interest, never sought her company, seemed to avoid the unconscious appeal in her eyes, and in fact generally emphasized that he preferred Cleo to Cathryn. Where she had once been his constant companion, now Cleo had taken her place by Dan's side. Her pillows were wet with tears at night and she lived with an ache in her heart but only to Peter did she betray her emotions. Outwardly, she was her usual self, light-hearted, innocently gay, sweet-tempered and keen to join in the entertainments which Peter provided for his guests.

Peter was her greatest comfort. Never a word of reproach did he speak because she had been such easy prey to the fickle Dan. If an awkward moment arose when they were all together, he was quick to cover it with a change of the subject or a suggestion which would take Cathy's attention away from Dan and Cleo. If she chose to excuse herself from any invitation, he did not press her, understanding her unhappiness and her reluctance to be hurt any more by Dan's obvious flirtation with Cleo. Subtly, he impressed upon her that he was loyal and only waiting for the chance to prove his love for her—that she could always depend on him and that he did not possess a fickle heart. Naturally charming to his guests, he nevertheless concentrated mostly on Cathy and she was grateful for his love and friendship. Bitterly she compared the two men, noting the values which Peter had and Dan lacked. But she could not retrieve her heart despite her words to Peter. Nothing would alter the love she had for Dan no matter how cruel and faithless he was proving to be. How mistaken she had been in him! She reminded herself that although he had spoken of love at first sight, he had never actually said that he loved her: they had never discussed a future which included them both; Cathy had to admit that Dan was not bound to her in any way. She had woven dreams about him in her heart so she suffered more now than if she had thought of him only as a passing affair, a brief flirtation, a sweet interlude. So while he hurt her, she readily forgave him for her longing could not be suppressed. She had given her love swiftly, impulsively—it was not his fault that he did not love her in return. She told herself that she was entirely to blame. She had made no secret of her love: perhaps he realized that he could never love her and, rather than hurt her in future, he had taken the opportunity which Cleo offered to point out to Cathy that she should save her love for someone more worthy of it. She did not think of this explanation immediately but it gradually came to her during the days which followed the arrival of the Vanneys.

One evening, on the way to dine at Chisholm House, she walked across the land which adjoined the two estates. As she entered the door, always unlatched, in the high stone wall which led to the flower gardens, she inadvertently caught sight of Dan and Cleo, locked in a passionate embrace, alone under the trees. She caught her breath sharply and paused with her hand on the latch, pain flooding her entire being. Anger and pain mingled to bring hot tears to her eyes—and then Dan released Cleo and turned to see her standing by the door. He looked startled and confused. She met his eyes for a long moment and then walked on towards the house, her vision blurred by tears but pride enabling her to keep her head high and her walk steady.

She heard Cleo's chiming laugh behind her, the low exchange of words and then she was out of earshot. She entered the house through the open windows of the drawing-room and found Peter talking to Noel, both men smoking cigarettes, drinks by their sides. Peter turned at her entry and greeted her warmly. Noel rose to pour her a cocktail.

Peter scanned her face, noting the tell-tale wetness of her lashes, the trembling of her lips. He glanced towards the garden. He had seen Dan and Cleo walk past the window some time earlier but had put little construction on the scene. Now he realized that Cathy must have seen them together and it did not take much imagination to know why she was so upset. He frowned slightly but did not mention her distress, drawing her round so that the light would not fall directly on her face and immediately breaking into conversation.

She sipped the cocktail, automatically replying to his remarks, gradually recovering her composure and grateful for his quick understanding and help.

Some minutes later, Dan and Cleo came into the house, hands linked lightly. She was looking up at him, speaking with animation, her words fetching an absent smile to his lips. But his eyes were not smiling and he instantly sought Cathy's face as she stood talking to Noel and Peter. She glanced at him and then, very pointedly, slightly turned her shoulder towards him and went on talking. No one else noticed the byplay but the little snub went deep into his heart although he knew that he was inviting her contempt.

Cathy could not remember a single detail of the rest of the evening when she was finally alone in her room, pressing her hot brow to the cool window-pane and letting her inner misery flow over her. There were no tears now: she was numb with the ache of despair. She visualized so clearly the scene she had witnessed: two bodies pressed together, dark head very close to the blonde hair, passion flowing between them. Once again she saw Dan's face suffused with guilt and surely there had been a hint of shame in his dark eyes. Cathy needed no clearer pointer to the futility of her love. But though she tried to summon contempt and scorn to her aid, first she had to battle with the pain and longing which possessed her.

CHAPTER 6

'Dan, I'm very annoyed with you!' Cleo spoke lightly but her eyes sparked with a brilliance which was very familiar to him.

He glanced at her quickly but his dark eyes were amused. 'Tell me the worst! What have I done?'

'You've made that poor child thoroughly miserable. I do wish you'd concentrate on mature women who know how to counteract your fatal charm.'

Dan flicked his lighter into life and she bent her head over the flame, drawing on the cigarette she had taken from the slim filigree case. 'Do you mean Cathryn?' His voice was very controlled.

'Yes—as *you* call her. I suppose that's another of your precious whims.' Her tone was scornful. His eyes flashed dangerously but he made no reply. 'Why don't you settle down with one woman and stop your rakish habits?'

'I haven't yet found the one woman I'd care to settle down with,' he replied curtly.

'Well, I think it's really too bad of you to play around with the affections of a little innocent like Cathy Ames.'

At this point, Cathy could not bear to hear any more. It had been by accident that she came upon them in the garden and she had paused at the sound of their voices. Their exchange of remarks had not made pleasant hearing to the girl they discussed. Now she moved forward but Dan spoke again and his words forced her to an abrupt halt.

'Oh, I admit I was only amusing myself—I didn't think she'd respond so readily.' His voice was a little rueful. 'I meant no harm but she's an impulsive, warm-hearted child—not cool and sophisticated like you, my dear.' He laughed lightly.

'You and I know how to fence words and glances, Dan my sweet,' she returned. 'I know well that you're never to be taken seriously—I'd never be fool enough to lose my head over you!'

'You're an experienced woman—Cathryn is a mere child ...'

'Is that her appeal?' Cleo cut in slyly, glancing at him through a thick veil of golden lashes.

'Appeal!' He repeated the word with deliberate light scorn for her benefit for it did not suit him at all for Cleo to discover that Cathryn's charms had woven a swift enchantment around his heart. 'I told you—it was for amusement only ...' He broke off as Cleo laid a warning hand on his arm and he turned round. Cathy came forward to join them, her expression giving no sign that she had overheard their conversation. She walked stiffly and her senses were numb but pride was strong in her and she managed to greet them casually.

She was wearing jodhpurs and white, open-necked shirt. The mass of auburn hair was pinned up into a neat chignon. She said easily, though her heart was rent with pain: 'You missed a fine ride—the horses were in really good form.'

'Too hot for me!' Cleo said quickly. She looked very cool and poised in a blue nylon dress with matching sandals. She swung sun-glasses in her hand as she turned to Dan: 'I could do with a long, cool drink, darling. How would you like to fix me one? I expect Cathy is hot and thirsty too, aren't you, my dear?'

She spoke kindly enough yet immediately Cathy felt that she looked hot and grubby and untidy. She flushed slightly. 'Peter and I have had a drink, thank you. He's mixing drinks for you two at the moment—that's why I came in search of you.'

'Darling, you go and collect them. I want to sit under that tree in the cool shade.' Cleo indicated a shaded spot which looked inviting in the heat of the afternoon.

Dan nodded. 'All right.'

Cathy walked back to the house with him for she meant to make her excuses and hurry home so that she could be alone with her hurt pride and grief. She could still hear the cutting remarks which Dan and Cleo had made. Let them think her a child—she knew that her love was that of a mature woman: let them think her innocent—she had no desire to be as experienced, as hard and brittle as Cleo Vanney, and innocence could be an appealing quality to finer men than Dan; the pain and anger were the outcome of Dan's admitted thoughtlessness and shallow cruelty in 'amusing' himself at her expense. Fine amusement indeed when it brought heartache and unhappiness to a woman he would probably never again give a single thought! What little depth there was to the man! It proved that charm and good looks were not enough and she had been a fool to be captured by these assets. She denied the prickling thought which whispered that it was his other qualities, the inner strength and courage, the warmth and sincerity, the innate goodness of his character, which had won her love for she had been given little proof that such qualities actually existed.

Dan looked straight ahead but he was very conscious of her silent nearness. Anxiously, he asked himself if she could possibly have overheard his conversation with Cleo—it was a sickening fear which increased as she made no attempt to speak to him. He would not have hurt her so for the world. His words had been meant for Cleo's ears, to kill any faint suspicion in her mind that he might care for Cathryn. He knew that Cathryn was unhappy and pained by his recent attitude towards her and it had been very hard to keep up the pretence. He recalled his words to Cleo, frowning slightly—if Cathryn had overheard him throwing her love in her face and dismissing her so lightly ... He could not continue the train of thought. His opinion of himself was low enough without adding such conjecture. No doubt Cathryn had walked straight out to them. He could not imagine her standing out of sight, deliberately listening to a conversation which was not meant for her to hear. So he reasoned to himself but a glance at her closed-in face did nothing to dispel his fears.

'I've decided to cut my stay short,' he said abruptly. 'I don't like to leave the estate for too long a time—particularly at this time of the year. I'm sure Peter will forgive me if I make my excuses.'

She forced herself to answer him although the sudden announcement had dismayed her. Firmly she controlled her trembling lips. 'Must you go?' she asked lightly. 'It's been a very pleasant break for us all, you know—new faces are always welcome in Buckhurst.'

He brushed this aside. 'I won't believe that my presence has made so much difference—you have so many friends that

I doubt if your life is ever dull.'

'Not exactly dull,' she admitted brightly. 'But I do get a little tired of the same set—Peter is the only one I never want to break away from.'

He glanced at her sharply. 'That sounds as if you've made up your mind to marry him, after all.'

She raised her chin. 'Perhaps I have. At least I know I can always trust him—and he does love me.' She spoke a trifle bitterly.

He laid a hand on her arm and drew her to a halt just out of sight of the house. 'You think that's enough?' he asked harshly. 'Don't you think it essential that you should love the man you marry?'

She drew her arm away from his fingers with a pointed movement. 'What makes you think that I don't love Peter?' she asked.

He paused a moment. Then, throwing all caution to the winds, he said quickly. 'Because you're in love with me. I'm not blind, Cathryn—and you've made no secret of your feelings.' He watched the swift colour surge into her face and his eyes were tender.

A brief hesitation, then Cathy said slowly: 'For a little while, I thought I did love you, Dan. But I'm very romantic and very impulsive. I realize now that you swept me off my feet but it was only infatuation. I've loved Peter all my life and I intend to marry him.' She lied to him bravely, too intent on concealing her own emotions to see the swift despair flash into his dark eyes.

He stared at her blankly. She spoke with real conviction and met his eyes without hesitation. He felt torn between the instinctive certainty that a mutual love had sprung to life at their first meeting and the reluctant acceptance of her innate honesty. He had to believe her words for he was sure that Cathryn would never lie to him or anyone.

He made a helpless gesture with his

hands, a slightly Continental movement which betrayed his Latin blood in the disturbance of his emotions. He longed to draw her into his arms and hold her close, to kiss her sweet lips until her eyes once again shone with the adoration they had held for him so recently. But there was no encouraging warmth in her eyes or attitude now. She was cool, aloof and very composed—it was enough to give him pause after one swift, impulsive step towards her.

He turned away, shrugging his broad shoulders. 'That's good news,' he said, forcing the words through stiff lips. 'I'm very pleased if only for Peter's sake—I know he's wanted to marry you for many years.'

They continued to walk towards the house and Cathy did not look at him as she said: 'We've always been so close—too close perhaps. I was so used to thinking of him as a friend and almost a brother that I didn't realize I wanted him as a lover and husband until it was almost too late.' The lies tripped from her tongue with ease—an ease which surprised her though she knew it was born of pride.

Peter came out of the house as they reached the stone terrace. 'Oh, there you are, Dan!' he exclaimed. 'There's a call for you from Norfolk—I've switched it through to the library in case it was private business.'

Dan nodded his thanks and cut through the french windows of the drawing-room on his way to the library. Peter glanced at Cathy and she forced a smile. She leaned against the stone wall of the terrace and looked over the flower beds beneath the raised paving. She had told Dan that she was going to marry Peter and this was indeed her intention. She knew Peter was still of the same mind and he would welcome the news that she was prepared to marry him. Cathy was determined to thrust Dan from her heart and memory and to concentrate on making Peter a good and loving wife. She was very conscious of his nearness as he stood beside her, smoking a cigarette, respecting her need of silence in those few moments. She felt a surge of affection for him and knew that he deserved all her love and consideration. Surely they could find happiness in marriage with such a firm foundation of long friendship and affection, mutual tastes, likes and dislikes, approval from both families, and their similar background.

But she could not speak of marriage yet to Peter. She needed a little time to renounce Dan completely, to impress upon her heart the futility of loving such a man and the need to forget his handsome good looks, his magnetic personality, the ardour of his embraces and the joy which had leaped in her entire being at her first meeting with the man who brought love into her life so swiftly.

When Dan rejoined them, his expression was grim and his dark brows were lowered. He did not look at Cathy. 'I'm afraid I'll have to race home,' he said quietly to Peter. 'My grandfather is very ill.'

Peter nodded, taking instant command of the situation. 'I'll tell Burrows to check over your car while you pack,' he said decisively. 'Cathy, go and tell Cleo the bad news and ask her if she cares to stay on here for a few more days or wishes to travel back by car with Dan. I'll find Noel.' Cathy sped away instantly, her generous nature sympathizing with Dan's obvious sorrow, the look of pain in his eyes and the tautness of his lips. Peter turned to Dan. 'Is he very bad?'

'Dying,' was the curt reply. He thrust a cigarette between his lips and flicked his lighter into flame. He inhaled the soothing smoke with thankfulness. 'I hate to rush off like this, old chap,' he said slowly, 'but I must admit I was thinking of cutting my visit short.'

Peter nodded. 'Understandable, in the circumstances,' he said evenly.

Dan laid a hand on his friend's shoulder

and smiled reassuringly into his eyes. 'I think everything will come about as you want, eventually, Peter,' he said quietly. 'Anyway, this is my cue to fade out of the scene and although there are many things I'd like to say to Cathryn, I don't mean to complicate matters further by saying them.' He sighed slightly. 'She's confused enough,' he added gently.

'I imagine you've accomplished what you set out to do,' Peter told him.

A wry smile twisted Dan's lips. 'No doubt I have. She now despises me thoroughly as a heartless, rakish wretch—certainly she'd never admit that she thought me wonderful when we first met! I can imagine the things she will say of me once I've left Buckhurst.' He gave a sharp, bitter laugh. 'Oh well, my shoulders are broad enough—the only thing that matters is her happiness and I believe she'll find it with you, Peter. Between you, you have everything to ensure a successful marriage.'

Peter raised his eyebrows. 'You seem convinced that Cathy will marry me—I wish I were as sure!'

Dan hesitated. If Cathy were not ready to tell Peter that she would marry him, then it was not his place to speak of it with certainty. So he merely said: 'I don't think you've anything to worry about, old man. Now I must go and throw my things into a suitcase.'

The Vanneys decided that they would prefer to travel back to Norfolk in the comfort of Dan's car and in a very short time they were exchanging farewells.

Dan and Peter shook hands with the warmth of long and sincere friendship. 'Thanks for everything,' Dan said quietly. 'I'll not see you for a while—the estate affairs will need my attention and it's better that Cathryn and I don't meet for a few months.' He spoke in a low voice which was only intended for Peter's ears.

An impulse stirred Peter to say: 'Look

here, old man—if you really care for Cathy ...'

Dan interrupted him sharply. 'Don't be a fool, man! Think of your own happiness, not mine. I can manage my life without anyone's help.' He turned away from Peter and bounded up the terrace steps to where Cathy stood, ready to wave them off. He gave her his hand. 'Goodbye, Cathryn,' he said gently.

She looked up into his dear face and her eyes softened. He had never been so dear to her now that she had renounced him for ever. 'Goodbye, Dan,' she replied with a tiny break in her voice.

He bent his head and brushed her cheek with his lips—a caress which brought a leap of joy to her heart. Then with a curt: 'Be happy, my dear!' he turned on his heel and ran down the steps to the waiting-car. She clenched her hands so tightly that her finger-nails dug into the palms and her eyes were hungry as they followed his tall masculine figure, loving the poise of the dark head with its rebellious waves and curls, the breadth of his shoulders, the nape of his neck with the attractive drake's tail of hair, the easy swing of his body and his lithe grace.

Dan swung himself into the driving seat and started the car. He sounded the klaxon in a last farewell and then the car moved off down the drive. He turned his head to catch a last glimpse of Cathryn and love mingled with despair in his eyes. He knew they would never meet again on a familiar footing. It was feasible that they would see each other but by then she would be married to Peter. Even if that wasn't the case, she wouldn't welcome his attentions with the open-hearted warmth which had first kindled the flame of love in his proud being.

Peter looked after the car and a slight frown marred his usually placid countenance. He wished he were as confident as Dan that Cathy meant to marry him. He was even more puzzled by Dan's strange behaviour. He apparently did care for Cathy but meant to do nothing about it—content to remove himself from her life as abruptly as he had entered it. Peter thought in passing of the long journey which lay ahead of Dan and his friends, and he wondered if Dan would arrive in Norfolk to find that he had succeeded to the title and estates of his grandfather.

He ran up the steps to join Cathy who had turned to enter the house with tears sparkling on her lashes and an ache in her heart.

Sensing her unhappiness, Peter said nothing. He linked his hand in her arm and they went into the hall together.

Afternoon tea was brought in to them and Cathy poured the hot, fresh liquid into the delicate cups. They talked occasionally but Peter was careful not to mention Dan until he felt she had recovered her composure.

Cathy spoke of Dan first. 'He seems very upset about his grandfather,' she said quietly. 'Was the news really bad, Peter?'

'I gather that the old man is dying,' Peter replied, lighting a cigarette. 'Still, he's had a good innings. I wonder how Dan will like his new title.'

'Title?' Cathy asked quickly.

'Didn't you know. His grandfather is Lord Ritchie, Ninth Earl of Carnaby. Dan becomes the tenth earl.' He looked at her in surprise. 'I'm sure I've told you that before.'

'Perhaps you have,' she said flatly. 'But I don't remember.'

'Oh well, it isn't important. Title or no title, Dan won't change very much.'

'He'll still make love to every woman he meets,' she retorted bitterly.

'Probably,' Peter agreed. He glanced at Cathy. 'I warned you against him,' he added quickly.

'Yes, I know.' She lifted her chin proudly. 'I was vain enough to think I might be the one woman who would really matter to him. But I soon realized my mistake. Now I'm beginning to wonder why he exercised his charms on me in the first place—after all, he obviously thinks me an inexperienced child!'

Peter crossed to sit beside her on the settee. He took her fingers in both of his strong, reliable hands. 'I hope you'll soon forget Dan,' he said slowly. 'I hope that you'll realize one day that the old love means more than the new, my dear ...'

She cut him short. 'If you really want to marry me, Peter—then I will.'

He was taken aback by the matter of fact tone of her voice. He looked down at her. 'Do you mean that?' he asked quietly.

She nodded. 'Yes, I do.' She turned slightly to face him and her eyes were honest and disarming. 'I won't pretend to you, Peter. I love Dan. I've never loved anyone before but I know that this emotion I feel is deep and real. I can't assure you that I shall soon get over it and learn to love you. In time, I expect, I shall be able to put my love in its right perspective. You've always meant a great deal to me, Peter—I can't imagine my life without you. If you're prepared to marry me, knowing that I love someone else but also knowing that I shall be faithful to you and do my best to make you happy, then I'm agreeable. But if you'd rather not have a wife on those terms, please say so and I shall understand.'

He was silent for a long time when she had finished speaking. Cathy did not urge him to a reply. Instead, she sat quietly, waiting patiently, fully aware that she was asking for something he might not be prepared to give but determined to make him happy if he wanted to marry her on these terms.

At last, Peter said: 'I'd marry you on any terms, Cathy, because I know that I can make you happy and that I can teach you to love me. But I want you to be really sure that you know what you're doing. Supposing Dan comes back into your life—as he will, you know—and your love is as strong as ever. What if he discovers that he loves you and comes to claim you once we're married? How will you react?'

Her voice was very bitter. 'That isn't at all likely to happen, Peter. I know that Dan doesn't care two hoots about me. But since you've raised the question, I give you my word now that nothing will induce me to break my marriage vows once I'm your wife!'

CHAPTER 7

They were married five weeks later.

Cathy had insisted on an early wedding as though she longed to close the door with finality on her chance of happiness with Dan. Peter was only too eager to agree to her wishes although it still seemed incredible to him that she meant to go through with the marriage. At times he paced his room, torn by the longing to see her happy even at the expense of his own hopes and dreams, mentally composing a letter which would bring Dan back to Buckhurst to claim the woman who loved him—then torn again by the love he knew for Cathy and his urgent desire to make her his wife. He could remember so vividly the instinctive love which had burst into bright flame between Cathy and

Dan. He could not deny his memory and at times he was tortured by visions of their mutual happiness, the joy they had shared in just being together, the look in Dan's eyes when he had promised to give her up so that Peter could one day marry the girl he had loved so long, and the grief and unhappiness which had destroyed some vital spark in Cathy.

While they discussed wedding arrangements, he studied her face and was anguished by the blankness, the lack of interest. He noted her hands, the restless, slim fingers entwining about each other. He looked in vain for some sign of the vital interest she had taken in life before Dan came to disturb her emotions.

One day, moved by an impulse stronger than his love, Peter asked her if she really wanted to marry him and assured her that he would understand if she had changed her mind.

She looked at him with a flicker of surprise in her lovely green eyes as though the idea of drawing back had not occurred to her—which it hadn't. 'If I marry you, Peter, I shall find a lasting happiness,' she replied and he could not doubt that she firmly believed this. 'No other man could be so loyal, so kind or so generous. I want to marry you, my dear—don't try to dissuade me.'

In the privacy of her own thoughts, Cathy admitted that marriage to Peter Wallis was an escape. Once she was his wife, she would repress the rebellious longing and love for Dan which dwelt in her heart. She felt something akin to love for Peter. All her life she had depended on him, loved and admired him, respected him in many ways, and assumed that one day she would marry him if only because they were so well-suited and it was the dream of their families. Now she told herself that he was by far the best man she could marry—reliable and understanding, kind and good-natured, loyal and true—all assets which she doubted that many men possessed. Even if Dan had returned her love and offered her marriage, love alone was no guarantee of happiness. Would they have shared so many interests? Their backgrounds were certainly different and their natures would have clashed, she was sure. Her love might have waned with the years of doubting his faithfulness, mourning his careless indifference to convention, searching in vain for the tender affection and swift understanding which Peter offered her instinctively. The love she knew for Peter had its foundation in years of friendship, and companionship, in the memories of shared and happy moments, in the approved union of two old and respected families. A touch of bitterness tainted the conclusive reminder that Peter wanted to marry her and Dan had only sought a brief entertainment, an amusing conquest, a swift enchantment which lost its interest, when it had gained its victim.

The colonel was delighted that his

hopes for his beloved daughter were to be realized. Peter's heart warmed at the reception of the news and it was very gratifying to know that he was accepted and approved by Cathy's family.

His own parents returned from a trip abroad only a few days after Dan and the Vanneys had left Chisholm House. They had been visiting his brother Graham who lived on the Continent with his wife and son. The news which awaited their return to Kent obviously completed the satisfaction they felt with their two sons who were proving their good upbringing by arranging their lives with good sense. They had always been very fond of Cathy Ames: their friendship with her family was of very long standing; they had approved the growing affection of Peter for Cathy throughout the years and had no objection to raise now against their marriage.

The wedding was very quiet for Cathy had wished it that way. They were married in the small church of St Paul in the village of Buckhurst and the vicar who conducted the ceremony had christened them both in that same small church. Bess and Diana were her attendants and for once Diana raised no outcry against the wearing of finery. It was a simple affair: Cathy wore the traditional white satin and lace and her veil was the same one which had graced her mother's head twenty-two years previously; she carried a white prayer book with a single white rose affixed to it. Her head was high as she walked down the aisle on her father's arm and if she longed to turn tail and run at this last moment, she repressed the longing and showed no sign of it in her demeanour. Peter's fingers clasped hers firmly throughout the service and she drew on his reassuring strength and the knowledge of his love. Her responses came clearly and without hesitation.

When they entered the church for the ceremony, the sky had been overcast though the day was warm. As bride and groom came out to be met with a flurry of confetti and cries of congratulations from the villagers, the sun suddenly burst through to smile benevolently upon the scene. Cathy raised her face to the sun and then smiled at Peter happily for it seemed a final blessing, a promise of happiness and the last doubt rolled away from her heart. Peter looked down at his lovely bride and his tender glance assured her of his love and his determination to make a success of their marriage despite its rocky beginning.

Although the wedding was a quiet and simple affair, the usual reporters appeared to take photographs and demand articles for their society magazines. Unexpected guests arrived on the scene and were made welcome by the colonel, who was only too pleased to show off his lovely daughter and assure everyone that in his opinion she could not have made a better choice. The Hall milled with people who overflowed into the gardens which were looking at their best on this sunny summer day.

Cathy found herself frequently parted from her new husband as she was surrounded by friends who plied her with eager questions. Peter too found himself carried off by his men friends who told him he was a lucky dog but that it was to be expected as he had never let another man within a yard of Cathy Ames.

Peter had sent Dan a card of invitation, dubiously wondering whether it were in the best of taste and yet hardly able to ignore the existence of the man who had been his greatest friend for some years. He received the expected letter of polite refusal but could not help a slight feeling of relief. Dan had explained that with the death of his grandfather, a great many responsibilities had devolved on his shoulders, and he was quite unable to leave them at the present time. He wished Peter and Cathy happiness and hoped to see them one day at his home in Norfolk.

Peter had given the letter to Cathy to

read. No expression flickered in her eyes as she scanned the page of bold, masculine handwriting. Calmly, she returned the letter and crossed Dan's name from the list of invitations. A few days later, they received a handsome wedding present from him and Cathy herself had undertaken to write the letter of thanks. Informal and pleasant though she made it, it was a difficult letter to write and she was glad that Peter was not with her to see the tears she brushed from her lashes.

Towards the end of the afternoon, Peter came in search of his bride, guided by the kindly directions of many friends. He found her with her father, the colonel's arm about Cathy's waist as they talked quietly together. They had slipped away from the milling throng for a last few words before he gave her finally into the protection of her husband.

'Cathy, isn't it time you went to change?' Peter suggested, glancing at his watch. 'The car is here and we are due to leave in fifteen minutes.' There was a note of authority in his voice which brought a smile to the colonel's lips. He liked a hint of firmness in a man's attitude to his wife and he was amused because Peter had so quickly adopted his new role.

'It's my fault, my boy,' the Colonel said easily. 'I wanted a few private moments with your wife before she left.' He touched Cathy's cheek with an affectionate hand. 'When she has changed, everyone will be crowding round to wish her luck and bid her farewell. You know, Peter, I'm a little reluctant to part with my girl although I'm damn pleased that she's married you.' He held out his hand to Peter. 'Be good to her, won't you!' There was a dryness in his voice which came from the depth of his emotions.

Cathy turned the moment swiftly. 'Daddy, you're not really losing me,' she reminded him. 'After all, I shall only be next-door, as it were.'

Chisholm House was quite spacious

enough to provide Peter and Cathy with a private suite and the arrangement had met with general approval. The colonel was pleased that Cathy would be living so near for it meant that she would be in and out of the Hall every day and he would scarcely know he'd lost her. Peter liked the idea for he had a great affection for his home. One day in the future, of course, it would be necessary to buy a house for himself and his wife but until that day came he was quite content to occupy a wing of Chisholm House which had been set aside for them. Cathy raised no objections. It suited her very well, for she could continue to stable her horses at the Hall in the kindly care of the groom who knew their every foible, she would be free to wander at random over the land which had been familiar to her from birth, she would not be suddenly uprooted from home and family and, apart from living with Peter as his wife and occasionally being called upon to entertain their friends, her life would scarcely be changed.

She left father and husband with a brief word of excuse and went up to her room to change. She wandered about the familiar surroundings, touching a loved piece of furniture, standing for a long moment by the window overlooking the familiar gardens, drinking in the beauty and the sunshine. At last, she sighed a little sigh, mentally girded her loins for the future ahead, and turned to the clothes that waited for her.

The ensemble she had chosen for travelling was a suit of coffee-coloured linen with cream accessories. The rich, glossy tresses of auburn hair were neatly brushed and twisted into a thick chignon which crowned her proud head. A dusting of powder over the small nose, a fresh trace of soft lipstick, a last glance at herself in the full-length mirror—then she was ready and she left the room where she had dreamed and hoped during the years of her youth—the room which had known her every mood, had received her confidences and absorbed her tears and laughter.

She slowly walked down the wide staircase to join her husband and she was unconscious of the presence of a new maturity which seemed to flow about her. Peter came forward to take her hand and then a crowd of well-wishers surged about them. It was some minutes before they reached the comparative security and peace of the waiting car. They moved slowly away to a last barrage of confetti, rose-petals and the gay, cheerful shout of their friends. Cathy looked back and saw her father, standing a little away from the crowd, his expression a little lost and sad. She felt a surge of warm affection as he raised his hand in a brief salute.

She sank back against the cushion and sighed.

Peter took her hand and squeezed her fingers. 'If that was a quiet wedding, I'm glad we didn't go in for a bigger affair,' he said with a smile. He glanced at her serious face. 'Tired, my love?'

'No. Just glad it's all over,' she replied.

They drove to a nearby private airport where a plane had been chartered to take them to Mentone in the South of France. Friends had offered them the use of their villa and they had accepted gladly. They planned to stay abroad for a month and included a visit to Graham Wallis in Paris in their itinerary.

The flight was pleasant. The sea sparkled in the sunshine as they crossed the Channel and it seemed a very short time before they were landing at Mentone. Peter had whiled the journey away with conversation and in retrospect they found many amusing incidents to laugh over with regard to their wedding. It was very comfortable, Cathy decided privately, to have married a man she knew so well for there was no tension between them only a familiar and pleasing intimacy.

Another car was waiting for them at the airport to take them to the villa.

They were greeted there by the English housekeeper who remembered them both from a holiday they had spent with their friends the previous year.

They dined alone and enjoyed their coffee in the warm evening air on the terrace. A pleasant walk about the gardens renewed their acquaintance with its beauty and careful cultivation. As the evening grew later, Peter suggested that they drive into the town where they could find a night-club for drinks and dancing to round off the day. Cathy agreed readily and changed into a flimsy chiffon dress of soft green. A stole and evening shoes completed her outfit and she joined Peter who had collected the car from the garage.

She sat beside him, watching the sea and drinking in the beauty of their surroundings as he drove along the road which ran parallel with the beach. She glanced now and again at his profile and her heart was warm with affectionate gratitude for his quiet understanding and the unselfish love he had always given her.

Only one thing marred the evening. They were sitting at their table in the night club, drinks before them, the dance music in the background, content with each other's company when a familiar figure threaded its way through the tables towards them.

'My dears, what a surprise! I was only saying to my friends that it's so deadly to be in a place and not know anyone there when I caught sight of you.' Cleo Vanney greeted them warmly and Peter rose politely to his feet. 'When did you arrive in Mentone?' she wanted to know.

'Only today,' Cathy replied. 'How are you?'

'Bored to death!' was the swift reply. 'I'm staying with the Chaillants—pleasant people but so dull! Are you here long? Perhaps we can get together.' She smiled upon them both.

'Cathy and I have just been married,' Peter told her.

'Then this is your honeymoon!' she exclaimed. 'Congratulations! Oh, but of course you'll want to be alone—I mustn't intrude on your privacy.'

'Won't you sit down and have a drink with us?' Peter invited politely.

'Well—only for a few minutes. I can't desert my friends for long.' She glanced across the room. Then she sat down between them and Peter snapped his fingers to a waiter. 'How well you're looking,' she told Cathy. 'Dan mentioned that you were getting married—isn't it rather sudden?'

'Not at all,' Cathy said smoothly. 'Peter and I have been practically engaged for years.'

Cleo smiled but she kept her thoughts to herself. 'It's a pity that Dan couldn't accept your invitation,' she said. 'But since his grandfather died, he's been rushed off his feet. I've seen hardly anything of him myself so I thought I'd take a little holiday over here and hope to find him less tied up when I get back. Hard work makes him so irritable, you know. It isn't like Dan to throw himself into estate affairs with so much energy.' She laughed. 'One could almost call him a reformed rake these days—except that it would be too disappointing if he had reformed!'

She rattled on in this strain for some minutes then at last she drained her glass and rose to her feet.

'It's time I left you newly-weds to yourself,' she assured them, kissed her finger-tips to them both and left them. Cathy watched the slim, elegant figure thread her way back to her friends and there was a hint of positive dislike and resentment in her eyes.

She turned to Peter. 'Shall we go?'

He rose immediately. 'Of course.'

They drove back to the villa and Cathy was very quiet. What stroke of Fate had determined that they should meet Cleo Vanney on this night of all nights? Her remarks had brought Dan so vividly back to mind and swift panic assailed her that she should never have married Peter while the very thought of Dan could cause such turmoil in her heart.

As though he read her thoughts, Peter said slowly: 'Most unfortunate meeting. The very last person one expects to run into over here—especially today!'

Cathy nodded. But she added oddly: 'I thought you liked Cleo Vanney?'

'I do. I think she's a really nice person beneath the social veneer.' He chuckled. 'You've never seen her as I have, darling—without make-up, hair disordered and in the oldest and most disreputable clothes in her wardrobe. We tramped for miles along the banks of a river and ended up by catching three different local buses to get back to Dan's place.'

Cathy made no reply and Peter glanced at her swiftly. Then he concentrated on his driving until they reached the villa.

While she lay in his arms that night and listened to the soft breathing of her husband as he slept, Cathy was grateful for the kind and gentle consideration which had made her wedding night less of an ordeal than she had expected. She had resolutely welcomed his embraces and responded to his passion, deliberately thrusting out all thought of Dan Ritchie. With Peter's lips on hers and his arms around her, she had given herself up to his love, blotting out the memory of Dan's ardent kisses, the powerful strength of his arms, the hardness of his body and the joy of his hands stroking her long auburn hair. But now that Peter slept, his fair hair rumpled and his face as innocent as a child's in slumber, sobs welled in her breast and silent tears scalded her cheeks as the memories came to emphasize the fact that her love for Dan was stronger than even she had suspected. Now she knew how wrong she had been to snatch at marriage with Peter. It would have been better never to have married than to live with this love in her heart for another man. Even time would not lessen the depth of emotion or erase the pain of her heart—yet her duty to Peter was very clear to her. He must never know that she regretted the step she had taken. She set herself the most difficult task of her life—to make her husband happy at all cost to herself and to teach herself to love him although it might not have the same qualities as her love for Dan. She would never know the rapturous joy, the swift surge of the heart, the tumultuous, heady rush of blood through her veins at an accidental touch of hands or a meaning glance. But a love of sweet contentment, of peace that comes from giving, of sincere affection growing into a rare warmth. Because it was Peter she had married—the dear, familiar companion of childhood and youth—it would not be impossible and surely the day would come when she would be able to think of Dan with faint nostalgia and mild warmth, happy in the assurance that she had created a marriage that was worthwhile and happy.

CHAPTER 8

Their honeymoon sped by, seeming all too short. The weather was delightful for the most part. They met some old friends and made many new ones: the villa was charming and a perfect setting; the days were long and full. Cathy enjoyed basking in the sunshine, although she was careful not to burn her sensitive skin. The sun brought out gleams of gold amid the auburn of her lovely hair and the scattering of freckles on her white skin were enchanting. They swam in the incredible blue of the Mediterranean: toured the countryside by car; enjoyed a mild flutter at the Casino. Cathy took a delight in scouring the quaint markets for unusual gifts to take home. She bought several new dresses and sandals and some costume jewellery. Peter seemed very contented and happy, and this was enough to ensure Cathy's own superficial happiness while she denied the grief in her heart.

They whiled away the days in lazy, pleasant fashion and all too soon they arrived in Paris to spend the last few days of their honeymoon with Graham Wallis and his wife. He was several years older than Peter and there was a marked resemblance in their looks and character. Graham had early developed a natural gift for painting and was making a name for himself in the art world. He had lived in Paris for some years and was married to a Frenchwoman. Gabrielle had been working as a reporter for a French newspaper when they first met. Graham's first exhibition had recently opened in Paris and her editor had sent Gabrielle to interview him. Graham had been captivated by her piquant looks, the bubbling sense of humour, the twinkle in her dark eyes and her knowledge of art. Their small son was now five years old, an enchanting mixture of French and English, and fluently bilingual.

Peter and his bride were made very welcome and there was no doubt that Graham and Gabrielle were delighted to accept Cathy into the Wallis family. Originally, they had intended to fly over to England for the wedding but Paul had unobligingly contracted measles. Now, however, all danger of infection was long past and the little boy considered his recent illness to be quite an achievement. He proudly boasted of the measles to Tante Cathryn within five minutes of their arrival at the Paris apartment. Paul was a precise little boy who always refused to shorten given names and it came as a slight shock to Cathy when he greeted her in this way. Wryly, she wondered if this were another unkind thrust of a fate determined to constantly remind her of Dan Ritchie. But she knew that many things would bring a reminder of him in the future and she must learn to hide her reactions and to accept the fact that memory was something which could never be denied existence.

The night before Peter and Cathy left Paris for England, Graham threw a lavish party for them on a scale which reminded Cathy of her father's reputation as a party-giver. For several hours the apartment swarmed with people who overflowed from room to room and out on the roof garden. It seemed to Cathy that she scarcely saw the same person twice for guests were constantly arriving and departing. Snatches of conversation floated into the air, drinks of all kinds were on tap, cigarette smoke wreathed up into the atmosphere and in a very short time Cathy's head began to ache slightly with the noise and the stuffiness. But she refused to take any notice of it and threw herself into the enjoyment of the evening which Graham had planned for their benefit.

Among the guests were several notable

artists: a husky-voiced and rather beautiful woman columnist who was a friend of Gabrielle's; an exiled Russian princess; one or two celebrities from the cinema world and a great number of the usually social-minded set who flitted from party to party with or without invitation.

Cathy left Peter in the clutches of the newspaper columnist and wended her way through the crowd to the open glass doors which led on to the roof garden. She glanced back to see Peter telegraphing an urgent signal to her to rescue him but she merely laughed and shook her head slightly. She found a drink pressed into her hand on one side and a handsome, blond young artist with a beard as blond as his hair offered her a cigarette. It was easier to accept than refuse so she took it and instantly he flicked a lighter into flame. He spoke to her and she replied politely, grateful that her French was fluent enough to pass unnoticed. The artist then proceeded to plunge into the interesting theme of art and nude models. His eyes were most expressive and his voice seemed to convey his admiration so, fearing that at any moment he might suggest that she would make a perfect model for his next canvas, Cathy hastily excused herself and left him to slip through the windows into the coolness of the evening. She looked about the pleasant gardens which successfully and discreetly concealed the fact that the apartment was set in a crowded and cosmopolitan area of Paris. Roof-tops nestled all around them but had been veiled by tall trellis-work with creepers entwined through the slats. Music came faintly from the room behind her mingling with the murmur of voices and laughter. She moved to lean against a parapet cut low in the high stone wall and she looked out over the square below. The apartment was at the top of a very high block of flats and in the distance she could see a portion of the Seine shining in the moonlight. The Eiffel Tower was also distinctively in sight, standing guard over the city which never slept while its famous river snaked its shining way to the countryside not far from Paris.

She stood alone for a few minutes in the peace and coolness, the freshness of the night air after the stuffy rooms of the apartment. Voices behind her caused her to turn round. A few yards away a couple were standing close together, talking in tones not so low that they were quite indistinct. But Cathy took no interest in their conversation. The man's back was towards her and its familiarity brought a shock to her heart. He was tall and dark, black hair waving riotously over a well-shaped, proud head: broad-shouldered, slim-waisted and narrow-hipped, he was immaculately dressed. Cathy's heart turned over and she involuntarily took a step forward. It was then that the man moved his head and his profile was turned towards her. A little sigh escaped her and she sank back against the parapet. There was no facial resemblance between the stranger and Dan Ritchie yet she could not deny that from the back he could easily have been Dan. Her reaction had shaken her and she stood trembling, trying to compose her thoughts and her thudding heart.

Peter's voice brought her swiftly to her senses and she turned a bright smile upon him. 'You're a fine one,' he accused. 'Running out on me like that—that vamp really had me cornered!' He looked down into her face. 'What's the matter?' he asked quickly, sensitive to her every mood. 'Are you feeling all right?'

She nodded. 'Yes, of course—I came out for a little air, it's so stuffy in there.' She took his arm and drew her to the parapet. 'Come and look, Peter—how I love this view at night. I wish I could take it home with me!'

'I must ask Graham to do a canvas of the scene,' Peter told her lightly. 'That's the only way you can take it to England, I'm afraid.' He slipped an arm about her shoulders and drew her head on to his shoulder. 'Happy, my darling?' he asked gently.

She nodded. 'Yes, Peter—very happy.'

He kissed her forehead with tenderness. 'No regrets?'

'None at all,' she assured him.

'You know, I'm rather looking forward to being home again,' he said lightly. 'We've had a wonderful time and I've enjoyed it immensely—yet I won't be sorry to return to Buckhurst.'

She teased him gently: 'You're English to the core, my dear Peter—no place like home, is that it?'

He smiled. 'With you every place is home to me,' he said softly and his lips were warm again on her brow.

She was touched by the remark and found it difficult to phrase an answer. So she turned towards him and raised her face for his kiss, her arms embracing him readily and warmly.

Their lips met. When Peter raised his

head, he rested his cheek on her hair and let his thoughts wander to the future with this beloved wife. Suddenly he tensed and then said, relaxing as suddenly as though with relief: 'Good lord! Cathy, do you see that man over there? Isn't he like Dan Ritchie until you notice his face? I had quite a shock for a moment.'

She turned and studied the man as if it were the first time she had noticed him. 'There's a vague similarity in build and height,' she said indifferently. 'But surely you didn't think it could be Dan?'

Peter laughed. 'One never knows. He's never in one place very long and it would be just like him to run over to Paris for a few days. There's plenty of people here who never received an official invitation and Dan would never miss up the chance of a party if he knew someone who meant to gatecrash—or even if he were visiting friends who had been invited.'

'Well, it isn't Dan,' Cathy said lightly and turned back to her favourite view of

Paris. She added easily: 'That would be too much bad luck—Cleo Vanney in Mentone and Dan Ritchie in Paris!'

Although she spoke lightly enough, Peter's eyes were troubled as he looked down at her, a slim figure in black velvet gown, a stole about her creamy shoulders, green eyes smiling up at him and the brightness of her hair completing the picture she made in the moonlight.

'But if by some chance he had been Dan—how would you have felt, Cathy?' he asked oddly.

'How would I have felt?' she repeated in order to give herself time to think. 'Pleased, I daresay—I've nothing against Dan.' She squeezed his arm. 'I was nice enough to Cleo, wasn't I? Yet I don't even like her!'

'You're evading my question very neatly,' he chided with a lightness he did not feel.

She hesitated. Then she said: 'Peter, if you're trying to find out whether I still care for Dan—then ask me outright. I don't like catch questions.'

He did not look at her. Staring over her bright head at the glistening Seine in the distance, he asked with a break in his voice: 'Do you still care for Dan?' It was of vital importance to him for he hoped desperately to have won her love during the last month. In every way, through the medium of speech, touch and senses, he had contrived to earn her generous heart. At times he knew the certainty of success for they shared a communion of spirit in rare moments which convinced him that he had erased the memory of Dan. But there were other times when Cathy seemed to recede from him, slipping into a world of dreams in which he did not exist, living a life in which he played no part—and it was then that Peter asked himself if she still thought of Dan and loved him despite everything. Again and again, he had longed to ask the question which he now forced through tense lips but always he had been afraid of the reply and it was this fear which prevented him from speaking the words. Now he waited in anguish, uncertain of her reply, conscious of the very slight hesitation in her attitude, dreading a destruction of his hopes.

Cathy drew a breath and expelled it in a tiny sigh. She hated lies of any kind, yet she knew that here a lie was necessary for she could not hurt Peter, so gentle, so patient and understanding. She knew his hopes and could not lightly toss them aside. So she lied. 'No, not in the way you mean,' she said slowly. 'I think I shall always be fond of him because he has such a warm personality and can be so nice underneath the bold and reckless exterior. But I don't love him, Peter. I never did. I realize that now—it was an infatuation of the moment.' She looked up into his eyes and added with convincing frankness: 'I love you, darling—now and for always. I've loved you all my life—but it took me a long time to discover that my feeling for you was love and not just friendly affection.'

Peter listened and longed to believe her, yet he knew instinctively that she was saying only what he wanted to hear. Her eyes betrayed her. The translucent and lovely green depths which were so expressive of her emotions. Now they failed to convey honesty although she did not realize it. She would not have raised her face so confidently to his gaze if she knew that her eyes spoke the truth while her lips lied. A surge of disappointment flooded him and pain mingled with resentment in his heart. He drew his wife into his arms and held her close without speaking, burying his face in the auburn mass of hair, while he struggled with his thoughts.

He knew that love was too delicate a flower to be forced. It could spring to life with startling suddenness—as it had with Cathy and Dan—or it could grow from a bud to ripening maturity slowly through the years—as with Peter. But nothing could ensure that the seed was planted by the gardener who searched for the blossom. Peter resigned himself to the truth that he lacked the enchanted spring to which the flower would reveal its heart. He must content himself with the little that Cathy could offer him and because he loved so much he was prepared to do this. He possessed her affection, her friendship, the companionship which they had shared so long, and the bonds of old and long-lasting ties. Many a marriage could be successful though love was one-sided and they had a great many other assets which some people lacked.

He understood too well the motives which had instigated her declaration of love. But he did not want to be *grateful* to the woman he had married nor did he invite her pity. But this reaction was only momentary and he firmly resolved to let Cathy think that he accepted her reply as the truth and never allow her to know that he was fully aware of the real state of affairs. She might love Dan still but she was not his wife and never could be—Peter told himself that he held the trump card—in his heart he could find a deep pity for the man and woman who loved but could never know happiness together.

Cathy stood in the protection of his arms and knew a peace steal over her heart because she had brought him a happiness she knew he had longed for. In marriage it was necessary that one should both give and receive—she had learnt that already—and Cathy found her greatest happiness in giving. She was sure that Peter had already found contentment in their marriage and this brought her a wealth of pleasure.

Some minutes later, they went back into the apartment to join the party which was still in full spate. They were talking to the blond, bearded artist and a few of his cronies when they were joined by the dark man who had caused Cathy such heart-burning. She discovered that he was a well-known French film actor. His colouring and build were identical with that of Dan Ritchie and there was a mischievous twinkle in his dark eyes which reminded her vividly of Dan but the lineage of his handsome face was vastly different. The conversation was adroitly switched from art to films and Cathy listened with interest, inserting a comment of her own occasionally. The actor, whose name was Vincent Despaid, glanced down at her with admiration in his dark eyes and complimented her on her excellent command of his language. Glancing at Peter, Cathy noticed a guarded look in his blue eyes and he moved towards her, slipping a possessive arm about her shoulders with a casual gesture. Cathy quickly repressed a smile at the action for it was typical of her husband if he thought that any man was showing too strong an interest.

The party broke up late and when they were finally on their own, Gabrielle made coffee and they sat talking and drinking the fragrant liquid, making the most of their last evening together, for Peter and Cathy were due to leave Orly Airport at ten o'clock the following morning.

The lounge door was suddenly pushed open and a fair, tousled head appeared. The little boy entered the room in his blue sleeping-suit, rubbing his eyes and very pleased to find his parents not yet in bed.

Cathy and Gabrielle exchanged laughing glances and then Graham swung his son up into his arms and demanded in mock reproof why he was not asleep in his bed. Gabrielle had tucked him up and left him sleeping innocently long before the first guests arrived. They would not have been surprised if the noise of the party had woken him earlier and he had investigated the cause of it for their guests were quite used to seeing a sleepy little boy come wandering into their midst.

Paul yawned and replied in French: 'It was so quiet that I woke up.'

There was a general chorus of laughter and he smiled cherubically. Cathy held out her arms to the child.

'Let me take him, Graham,' she suggested.

Paul went willingly for he had readily given his affection to Tante Cathryn who had always shown him a loving and kindly tenderness. She had an instinctive way with children which Peter had observed and appreciated for it was his dearest wish that they should in time have children of their own. She cradled him on her lap and he snuggled up to her, enjoying the unexpected nocturnal attention. For a little while she concentrated on Paul, talking to him and promising that one day, when he was older, he should come to England to stay with them. Gradually, his long dark lashes fluttered sleepily and eventually nestled on the round curve of his cheek, hiding the dark eyes he had inherited from Gabrielle and which were such a sharp contrast to the fair curls. Cathryn rose carefully to her feet and carried him back to his tiny bed where she settled him, smoothing the pillows and straightening the blankets which were in turmoil from his restless slumbers. Peter followed her from the lounge and stood by the nursery door, leaning against the post, watching his wife with an enigmatic expression in his eyes. She was quite unaware of his presence as she stroked the fair curls back from the intelligent brow and looked down on the innocent babyish face. He was like enough to his father to remind her vividly of the photographs of Peter as a small boy and she was thinking that if one day she had a son he would probably resemble very much this half-French cousin. There was a strong maternal streak in her being and she wanted children. Also, she knew that it would bring a new happiness to her marriage and create a stronger tie than ever between Peter and herself.

It was a long time before they slept that night, for she lay in her husband's arms and they found many things to say to each other. In the intimacy of the night, Cathy often opened her heart to Peter and he welcomed her confidences. But there were some things deep in her heart which she could never reveal no matter how close they might be and he sensed this. There were times when she clung to him, longing with all her heart to tell him how deeply she yearned for Dan but how resolved she was to put him out of her mind and bring happiness to the man she had married—but she resisted the impulse and only the tension of her slight body told him of the emotions which ransacked her. Then he would hold her very close and be very tender so that she drew some comfort from the assurance of his love.

This night, there was no passion in their communion—only a great sweetness and a sense of peace as she again offered him

the opportunity to believe her declaration
of love and with resignation of spirit but
a true understanding of her motives he
assured her of his belief.

CHAPTER 9

Cathy surveyed herself in the full-length mirror and approved her appearance. Peter came in from the bathroom in his dressing-gown, his fair hair wet and rumpled.

'That's nice, darling,' he approved.

Cathy swung round to show off her gown. 'Do you really like it?' she demanded. They were going to a ball and she had bought her dress from one of the leading London *couturières*. The simple Grecian lines suited her slim figure and clung to the contours of her body: the colour was hard to define being a smoky confusion of grey, green and blue, but there was no denying that it suited her rich colouring and creamy skin; it flowed and swirled about her as she moved with natural innate grace and Peter crossed to cup her face in his hands and kiss her parted lips with gentleness.

'You're beautiful,' he assured her quietly and she thrilled to his generous praise.

They were staying at the London flat which was the base for all town activities for the Ames family and Cathy was welcome to continue to use it when she and her husband spent any time in London. This ball was the beginning of a round of social life which heralded the advent of Christmas.

Many invitations had been received and the majority of them accepted for Cathy had a suspicion that when the end of the following summer came she would have a welcome tie which would mean the end of her social life for a little while. She had not yet told Peter that she hoped she was carrying now the child he so ardently longed for but there was no doubt in her mind and she was thrilled with the prospect.

Peter was soon ready, looking very well

and handsome in the white dinner jacket and tie with the black evening trousers. With a wifely air she surveyed him, slightly straightened his tie and suggested that they should leave for the ball.

It was a large affair, held at a big Mayfair hotel, and their hosts were old friends who made them welcome and assured them that marriage seemed to agree with them both. Champagne flowed and the music invited them to join in the dancing which was already well under way. They found a table and were very soon surrounded by young friends. Their party was a gay one and Cathy enjoyed herself, leading the conversation at times, her light laugh often infecting the others. She loved dancing and never lacked for partners. Compliments flowed as freely as the wine and she seemed to blossom underneath the admiring gazes of the young men who sought her company. Peter was very proud of his young and lovely wife and was quite content to relinquish her to the arms of their friends who wanted to dance with her, to listen to her merry conversation and her infectious laugh, to watch her expressive face with its swift changes and to give her his loving admiration.

She was sitting at the table with her glass in her hand, listening to an amusing story which kindled her eyes with laughter and curved her lips with a sweet humour when suddenly a strange instinct drew her attention from her companions and she looked over their heads into the dark eyes of Dan Ritchie. Her heart missed a beat and she caught her breath sharply for he was the last person she had expected to meet. He was watching her, standing alone by a marble pillar, tall and powerful, handsomely arrogant. Fleetingly she wondered why he had not approached their table and made his arrival known to them. When their eyes met, he smiled and nodded his head in acknowledgement. A slight shiver ran through her entire body and then, with a brief word of excuse, she rose to her feet and walked towards him, quite unaware that Peter turned to watch her progress and stiffened at sight of Dan. She was oblivious to everyone else but Dan and it was as though his very presence bewitched her.

He waited for her and then his hands met and held her eager, responsive fingers. 'Hello, Cathryn,' he said, and the vibrant richness of his voice thrilled her enchanted heart.

'I didn't know you were in London,' she said and stumbled on the words.

'A brief holiday,' he explained. 'How are you, my dear? You're looking very well and extremely beautiful.'

She smiled her thanks. 'It's wonderful to see you, Dan,' she said sincerely, not caring that her heart was in her eyes for him to see. She forgot the cruel words she had overheard, forgot his fickle treatment of her, was conscious only of the love for him which was as strong as ever and flamed quickly at sight of him.

'I've neglected you shamefully,' he said with a rueful smile. 'I should have paid you both a visit long ago.' He looked past her and nodded to Peter who still watched, his eyes troubled, his whole attitude one of tension. 'I mustn't keep you from your friends,' he said slowly. 'Let me escort you back to your table, Cathryn.' He released her hands and she turned to walk with him.

Peter waited silently. Their friends continued their conversation, barely noticing his sudden withdrawal and quite oblivious to the undercurrents which permeated the little scene enacted behind them.

Dan gave Peter his hand. 'Good to see you again, Peter,' he said warmly. Peter rose and shook hands, while Cathy sat down at her place, watching them but still bewitched.

Peter swiftly introduced Dan to his companions and then said easily: 'Won't you join us, Dan—or are you with a party?'

Dan pulled out a chair and sat down beside Cathy. 'I'm alone, as a matter of fact. Thanks, I will join you.'

Conversation became general and with an effort, Cathy shook off the enchantment which Dan's presence bound about her, and entered into the spirit of the party once again. She flashed a quick, repentant glance at her husband and wondered how she would explain her flight to Dan's side when they were alone. Peter met her eyes levelly and then turned to talk to Dan. To a casual observer, he appeared completely at his ease and well-pleased at the arrival of his friend, but Cathy knew him so well that she sensed the hurt he endeavoured to cover with light raillery. Regret mingled with joy at seeing Dan again, having him so close to her, being able to listen to his charming voice and watch his handsome face as he talked. She did not try to explain the instinct which had told her of his presence or the strange impelling force which had taken her immediately to his side. For the moment, she pushed aside all thoughts of consequences and concentrated solely on the pleasure of having him near.

Dan invited her to dance with him, first cocking an impudent eyebrow in Peter's direction and saying lightly: 'Do you mind if I dance with your wife, old man?'

Cathy went into his arms and gave herself up to the exquisite joy of his near intimacy. They danced well together, their steps matching, their bodies seeming to merge into one.

Dan had never ceased to love his Cathryn but he had long since resigned himself to life without her. If any hopes had lingered, they had been destroyed when she married Peter. But now a devil of mischief had entered his soul and he tossed aside all discretion, determined to enjoy the gift which the gods had offered him, and prepared to know an evening of enchantment in Cathryn's company. He had been startled by her increased beauty, by the lithe grace of her movements, by her obvious welcome and an imp whispered in his ear that though she might have married Peter, she was still in love with him. As love sprung to life again, resignation vanished and he asked himself why he had given her up so easily when all her beauty and warmth and generous nature could have been his to possess. His blood surged hotly through his veins as he held her in his arms and he thrust aside the thought that she was now another man's wife. He had never cared for convention, could be unscrupulous and reckless when he chose, and it was only his firm belief that Cathryn deserved a better fate than marriage to a man like himself which had prevented him claiming her in the first place. Now he was on fire for her and his passion urged him to take her from Peter, to snatch at a momentary if not a lasting happiness, to know the joys and the sweetness of her love.

He held her very close and her silken

hair brushed his cheek. He looked down at the curve of her cheek, the fan of lashes sweeping in beauty across that curve, the tilt of her small nose and the generous, sweet mouth.

Not a word had been exchanged since they rose to dance. But now he said softly: 'How beautiful you are, my Cathryn. Is it the maturity of marriage or the restlessness of an unsatisfied heart?'

She glanced up at him quickly, defensively. Had she imagined a trace of mockery in his tone? 'I'm very happy,' she said quickly.

He chuckled. 'That isn't what I asked you. But I won't tease you, my sweet. Tell me about your honeymoon—Cleo Vanney told me that she met you in Mentone. Did you have an enjoyable stay there?'

'Yes, thank you.' She flushed slightly for she felt that he was deliberately making her feel young and *gauche* when in fact she was a mature and sophisticated woman.

As though he read her thoughts, he

said with a laugh: 'What happened to the sophistication you once displayed to me, Cathryn? You're like a bewildered child lost for words—do I have such a frightening effect on you?'

The music stopped and she was saved the necessity of a reply. She turned to walk back to their table but he stopped her with a hand on her arm. 'Cathryn, don't rush back to those morons. I want to talk to you. Can't we find a quiet corner by ourselves where we can have a drink and toast our chance meeting?'

She looked up at him and his dark eyes were smiling down at her. She nodded, a little reluctantly. 'Yes, if you like.'

They found a recess in the corridor which was cut in the wall. A comfortable couch was standing there, conveniently empty, and a waiter hovered nearby.

'Perfect!' Dan commended. 'I might have ordered it like this, don't you agree?'

'Perhaps you did,' she replied lightly, sitting down and arranging the folds of her skirt with hands that trembled slightly. She was nervous not from fear but from excitement and happiness.

Dan ordered champagne and then sat down beside her, half-turning in his seat so that he could study her lovely face. With a quick movement, he captured one of her slim hands and lifted it to his lips. Cathy snatched it away.

'Please don't!' she said quickly.

He raised a quizzical eyebrow. But he merely said: 'You can't imagine how pleased I am to find you here, Cathryn. I've thought of you so often.' He smiled ruefully. 'I'm afraid you made a great impression on me when I was staying with Peter.'

She raised innocent eyes to his, her lips a little tremulous. He caught his breath and would have pressed his ardent mouth against her lips at that very moment if the waiter had not interrupted them with the wine. Dan gave him a curt word of thanks and waited impatiently for the man to withdraw. But this respite gave Cathy a chance to pull herself together, to recall his conversation with Cleo Vanney and to remind herself that he was once more exercising his charms only for amusement. When he turned back to her, she was completely in control of the situation, a little smile flickering about her lips, her eyes amused but guarded.

'I should imagine that all women make a great impression on you, Dan,' she retorted lightly. 'I don't think I should place too much importance on that statement.'

His dark eyes met hers levelly. 'You've sized me up, haven't you?' he asked with a laughing glance.

She nodded. 'I have indeed. You made a fool of me once, Dan Ritchie—it won't happen again.'

He was puzzled. 'What do you mean? How did I fool you?'

'That isn't what I said,' she responded. She touched his hand lightly with her fingers. 'I know very well that you set out to blind me with your charms while you were staying with Peter. Surely I wasn't the only available girl you could practice on?' She gave him a quizzical look. 'But I think I led you to believe that I took you seriously—a little scared, you dropped me very quickly when Cleo Vanney arrived. I find it rather amusing in retrospect.'

He was silent a moment. Then he shook his head. 'A very good effort, Catherine—but not really convincing. Confess that you fell in love with me then and only married Peter because I hurt your pride by turning to another woman at the first opportunity.'

A faint flush stained her cheeks. 'I don't think that effort is very convincing either,' she retorted. 'It certainly isn't true.'

'Well, I'll concede that your motive for marrying Peter might have been different—but I'm damn sure that you fell in love with me.' He added gently: 'I'm just as sure that you still love me, my Cathryn.' He raised her chin with his fingers and looked into her eyes. 'Confess it,' he urged.

She wrenched her head away. 'I wouldn't give you such satisfaction—even if it were true.' She lifted her glass of champagne. 'You wanted to toast our unexpected meeting—here's to it!' She drained the glass and rose to her feet. 'Now we must go back to the ballroom—Peter will be anxious about me.'

He stood up obediently but his eyes searched her face and he caught her hand swiftly. She glanced at him, surprised by the impulsive movement.

'No,' he said slowly. 'You won't admit it—but I know you love me. You're married to Peter and there's a streak of stubborn loyalty in you, my Cathryn.' He sighed.

'Stubborn loyalty?' She raised her eyebrows as she repeated the words. 'I should have said—natural loyalty. Yes, Dan, Peter is my husband and I'm very happily married—I would appreciate it if you make the effort to remember that in future.'

She withdrew her fingers and walked away from him. After a moment, he hurried after her and with a hand on her shoulder, he swung her round. His hands were insistent and urgent as he drew her close, his eyes compelling her surrender. Her heart began to thud unevenly and she forgot everything but his nearness. Her body thrilled to his touch and her lips parted instinctively to receive his kiss. His mouth was warm, gentle but eager. Cathy's senses swam as she stood in the circle of his arms and responded with all her generous, impulsive heart to his ardent embrace.

When he finally released her, she raised stunned eyes to his face. His smile was reassuring and faintly triumphant. She took a step back, horrified at her easy submission and swift response. Anger surged through her, mainly directed at herself but partly directed at Dan. She raised her hand and dealt him an angry slap. The slap resounded and he paled under the blow, the weals standing out redly on his cheek. For a moment he struggled with his self-control then suddenly he laughed lightly.

'How very conventional!' he mocked. 'Do you really think that Peter will believe you were an unwilling party to our embrace if I return to the ballroom with the marks of your fingers on my cheek?'

Cathy was trembling. She had instantly regretted the blow and her own loss of temper and she longed to take his beloved face between her hands and kiss the weals she had caused. But she did not dare. His eyes were steely despite the light tone of his voice and a tiny nerve jumped in his cheek to betray his inner anger.

'I'm sorry,' she said slowly. 'That was unforgivable.'

As a crowd of young people came into the corridor at that moment, surging from the ballroom, Dan put his hand beneath her elbow and they walked towards the main doors which stood wide open. A casual onlooker would not have noticed the tension between them.

Dan said easily: 'The marks will fade and as your motive was perfectly obvious, then you are easily forgiven. It isn't the first time I've had my face slapped, I assure you—'

'I can believe that,' she put in dryly.

'I consider your reactions quite a compliment,' he went on, ignoring her remark.

She drew a sharp breath. 'I don't understand you.'

'Really?' The mocking note was back in his voice. 'Come now, Cathryn—you don't expect me to believe you. You know as well as I do that you slapped me in temper. You're angry because you responded so readily to my kisses. It was a complete give-away—rather a contrast to your cool explanation that you were merely playing up to my attentions when I was in Buckhurst! You've admitted that you love me ...'

She interrupted swiftly: 'I said no such thing!'

He smiled. 'Words are sometimes unnecessary, my dear. As I was saying, you feel guilty about loving me when you're married to Peter, so you instinctively hit out as a defence against your own vulnerability. The primitive female urge, I suppose.'

'What is?'

'To want to punish someone else for your own guilt,' he replied smoothly.

'Quite the psychologist, aren't you?' The words held a sneer. She resented the truth of his remarks and was angry again because he had knocked down so deftly the flimsy barrier she had tried to erect.

He shrugged. 'I've studied women for many years,' he said with a twinkle in his dark eyes.

'That's very obvious!' she retorted. 'After all, you have quite a reputation, haven't you, Dan?'

As though it were an interesting fact which he had just discovered, he said smoothly: 'You're very beautiful when your eyes sparkle with anger and your cheeks flush so prettily with temper.'

'You're impossible!' she snapped and walked into the ballroom with her head high. She heard his light laugh behind her and despite her annoyance, her own lips curved slightly in a smile for she too could appreciate the amusement which lay in their exchange of words. But she did not turn her head, very conscious that he walked only a pace or two behind her.

Peter was dancing with one of the girls from their party and as Cathy and Dan passed by, he flashed an enquiring glance at his wife. She smiled at him warmly, repressing the guilt which his glance brought to her heart.

For the rest of the evening, she was aloofly polite to Dan and assiduously affectionate to Peter. He said nothing about their absence from the ballroom though his brain seethed with questions. His heart ached with the knowledge that Cathy's feelings had not changed in the least where Dan was concerned. Although he had known it even when he married Cathy and since, despite her repeated assurances that she loved him and Dan had only been a passing infatuation, reminder of the fact that one glance from Dan's dark eyes could enchant her to the oblivion of everyone and everything else was very painful. He could not guess what had passed between them during the time they had been away but his eyes quickly detected the fingerprints on Dan's cheek and this surprised him very much. But he made no comment and the weals quickly faded.

Dan left the party before it finally broke up. Saying goodnight, he promised to get in touch with Peter and suggested dinner for the following evening at a night club. Peter glanced at Cathy for guidance but she turned to her neighbour with an eager comment as though the invitation was of little interest. So Peter merely replied that they could discuss it when Dan telephoned, adding that Cathy knew better than he did what engagements they had already accepted. Dan accepted this with a little nod, bade a general farewell and crossed the ballroom without a backward glance.

CHAPTER 10

Because Peter did not mention her absence with Dan, guilt weighed heavily on Cathy's heart. During the drive back to the flat and as they sat over coffee before going to bed, she waited, dreading yet expecting the questions she was sure he would ask. But none came. He spoke only of the ball, of their companions, of the success of the evening, casually of Dan's unexpected presence and his hope that they would see him again before he returned to Norfolk.

Cathy stirred her coffee thoughtfully. 'You're very fond of Dan, aren't you?' she said slowly.

Peter smiled a little. 'Well, a man doesn't say that kind of thing,' he returned. 'Dan and I have always been the best of friends ...'

'That's what I mean. It's a pity that he lives so far from us—I expect you'd like to see him more often.'

'I would,' Peter admitted. 'But life changes, you know. After all, I'm a married man now and you're always my first consideration. We have a long-standing invitation to Norfolk but I hesitate to suggest that we pay him a visit because I don't think you'd be happy there.'

She glanced at him swiftly. 'Why not?'

He shrugged. 'Cleo is still very much on the scene, I imagine—and you didn't like her. Dan and I would bore you to death with our talk of the good old days at college and our experiences together. The nearest big town is several miles away and one rather relies on the locals for entertainment ...'

Cathy said: 'It sounds very much like Buckhurst.' She added without looking at him: 'The real reason hasn't been mentioned yet, Peter.'

'Which one?'

She flashed him a reproachful glance. 'Don't pretend to me, Peter—I mean my old infatuation for Dan and you know it.'

He rose and began to pace the room restlessly. 'It isn't really old, is it, Cathy?' She made no reply and after a moment he went on: 'I'm not blind, you know, my dear. When you saw Dan tonight, nothing would have stopped you from going to him.' He sighed.

She ran her hand over her hair in a gesture of despair. 'I'm sorry, Peter,' she said dully.

He stopped pacing and regarded her affectionately. 'You've never deceived me for one moment, Cathy. I've always known that Dan is the only sun in your sky—oh, I appreciate your efforts to make me believe otherwise. I know you did it with good intent. I know you wanted me to be happy.' He crossed over to her and sat down beside her, taking her hands. 'I have been happy,' he said in a low voice. 'When you know that you'll never have everything, you content yourself with a little, darling. You've been a wonderful wife to me ...'

She turned to him and put her arms about him, holding him close, her face buried in his shoulder while the tears flowed unchecked. If only she could love Peter who was so good and generous and loving ... If only she could thrust Dan from her heart and deny the hungry longing which was her constant companion ... If only ...

He let her cry while he held her tightly, his lips against her rich, silken hair. He loved her so much. But he realized now that he should never have married her. He should have done everything in his power to bring Dan and Cathy together, to bring about a marriage between them even if their happiness had been short-lived. He had thought he was doing the right thing but while Cathy's heart could ache and her tears flow like this, he knew that her only happiness lay with Dan and he sacrificed his own love and longing and the need of her.

After a while the storm abated and he continued to hold her against his heart, stroking the vital, thick strands of her auburn hair, murmuring words of comfort as though she were a child.

He said gently: 'It will break my heart to lose you, Cathy—but I'll give you your freedom. I won't stand between you and Dan any longer ...'

She raised her head to look at him with startled eyes. 'What do you mean?'

'Dan loves you, Cathy,' he replied quietly.

She repeated the words with amazement. 'Dan loves me?'

He nodded. 'Yes.'

She clenched her hands in agony. 'How do you know?'

'We talked it over once. Dan admitted that he loved you. He knew too that you loved him. But he knew that the little he could offer you would never be enough to ensure your happiness ...'

'The little he could offer me?' She was stunned, incredulous. 'But if he loves me ...? Peter, that would be everything—I wouldn't ask for more. I wouldn't care what the future held ...' She broke off. A moment later, she said dully: 'No, Peter. I know differently. Dan has never loved me. I heard him talking to Cleo Vanney—he said then that he was only amusing himself with me, that he wanted to prove that he could still make a conquest. Don't try to make things easier for me, Peter—I've always known that my love for Dan is hopeless.' She sat up, drawing her arms from him, and her green eyes were despairing.

'Is that why you married me?' Peter asked slowly. 'Because you overheard Dan talking nonsense to Cleo? Did you expect him to admit to her that he loved a sweet and innocent girl—that he really loved for the first time in his life—that he was prepared to give up his own happiness so that he shouldn't destroy her illusions in his goodness, his sincerity, his warmth and fineness? Dan knew what he meant to you ...'

'I thought I meant the same to him,' Cathy said slowly.

'Well, you did! Believe me, Cathy. Dan has never lied to me—and his love for you was the greatest thing that ever happened to him.'

There was a long silence. Peter took a cigarette and lit it with trembling hands. He was throwing away his own happiness—giving his wife the chance of marrying Dan—supporting Dan's suit and emphasizing his good points ...

Cathy thought of his words and a ray of hope pierced her heart. Dan loved her—he really loved her and had wanted to marry her. If she had not rushed into marriage with Peter ... But Peter offered her freedom—a thought struck at her with icy shock. Beneath her heart she carried Peter's child and this was a tie more binding than any marriage ceremony. She could not break up their marriage to find happiness with Dan when she had Peter's child to consider. She would never forgive herself if she betrayed not only the man she had married but her own unborn baby. How could she live with the knowledge of her own selfishness? It was not in her nature to disregard her duty to Peter and his child. They had more claim on her than Dan could have—more claim that her own search for happiness. She had been reasonably happy during these last few months—she had found contentment in her marriage—peace had come to her with the knowledge that Peter's love and loyalty throughout the years had not been in vain. The ray of hope died a swift, instantaneous death and her resolve to continue with her marriage and to deny Dan and his love was strengthened.

She had reached this conclusion when Peter said gently: 'It shouldn't be too difficult to arrange a divorce, my dear—I'll supply you with the necessary evidence and when the whole unsavoury business is over, you can marry Dan and be happy. All I want is your happiness, Cathy ...'

She shook her head. 'No, Peter.'

He was startled. 'What do you mean?'

'I don't want a divorce,' she said firmly.

He raised her fingers to his lips. 'Darling, it's time you stopped considering me. Believe me, I shall be happier knowing that you've found happiness than if I keep you tied to me knowing that you want Dan with all your heart.' He smiled a little crookedly. 'Don't try to stop me from being the gallant, Cathy—it won't hurt me to be unselfish for once in my life!'

'I don't want a divorce,' she repeated.

'But—why not?' He was truly dumb-founded.

'Because I've no wish to marry Dan,' she replied with a slight tremor in her voice. 'I think we'd be totally unsuited for marriage.' She forced a little laugh. 'I can't help being mesmerised by him whenever we meet—but that doesn't mean that I have to break up a perfectly good marriage which has been proving very successful.' She turned to him eagerly. 'You've been happy, haven't you, Peter?'

'Yes, but ...'

'Then I want you to go on being happy. I've found my happiness in being with you, Peter ...'

He rose abruptly to his feet. 'I'm sorry, Cathy—but there's something else behind this decision of yours. I firmly believe that you love Dan and want to marry him so tell me why you won't take the chance I'm offering you.'

She raised her head and met his eyes levelly.

'Very well. I'm going to have a child, Peter.'

There was a stunned silence as he searched her face for confirmation. But the truth shone from her eyes and understanding flowed over him immediately. Understanding and an instinctive agreement with her decision and the arguments which had cemented it.

He said at last: 'That puts a very different complexion on matters, of course. Are you sure?'

She shrugged. 'I haven't yet had confirmation, if that's what you mean. I'm sure enough.' This was so different to the way she had planned to break the news to him and her heart ached for the dreams she had woven.

He said helplessly: 'I'm sorry—I never meant this to happen ... I wanted children but not so soon ...' He broke off for she leaped to her feet and pressed her fingers against his lips.

'Don't say such things, Peter!' she urged him. 'Can't you understand— I'm glad about the child! I'm really glad!'

He caught her close to him. 'Do you mean that?'

She nodded. 'Of course I do. Children are one of the blessings of marriage and I know that there will be many other blessings in our marriage.'

He kissed her brow gently. 'You're a brave and wonderful person, Cathy,' he said sincerely.

She laughed into his eyes. 'I'm also a very determined person,' she told him, 'and I mean to make a success of our life together.'

'And Dan?' he asked quietly.

She paused while a flicker of pain crossed her eyes. 'Dan will always be very dear to me,' she said with a break in her voice. 'But you're my husband and I love you—even if I keep a place in my heart for Dan.' She added wisely: 'God has His own plans for our lives, Peter—we can't deviate from the path He chooses and time always proves that His plans are the right ones.'

He kissed her with great tenderness and love. There was peace in her heart and the joy which comes from unselfish giving and the willingness to part with a cherished dream when reality signposts a different if difficult path.

Another engagement prevented them

from dining with Dan the following evening and he telephoned two days later to tell them that he was returning to Norfolk. He asked if he could call to see them before he left and Peter turned to Cathy with a question in his eyes.

'Dan wants to come up before he goes back to Norfolk,' he said.

'Tell him we'll be very pleased to see him,' she returned immediately, glancing up from the flowers she was arranging artistically in a jardiniere.

Peter passed on the message and then, after a brief exchange of remarks, replaced the receiver. 'He's on his way now,' he said. 'Do you really want to see him?'

She met his eyes squarely. 'Of course I do.' She smiled. 'He's my husband's greatest friend.'

When the doorbell pealed, Cathy herself went to admit Dan. He stood, tall and handsome, smiling down at her. She invited him in and closed the door behind him, as Peter came out of the lounge with hand outstretched. The two men shook hands and then Cathy said lightly: 'I'll order some tea—or do you prefer something stronger, Dan?'

He shook his head. 'Too early,' he replied. 'Tea will be much appreciated.'

Over tea they talked of many things and Dan touched again on the subject of their visit to Norfolk. 'I should like you to see my home,' he said to Cathy. He turned to Peter. 'I've made a few improvements since my grandfather died. You'd be interested to see the changes. When are you coming to stay with me?'

Peter and Cathy exchanged glances. Then Cathy said: 'We'd love to come. I'll leave it to Peter to make the arrangements.'

Dan grinned. 'He's a shocker at writing letters—still, I hope you'll make it fairly soon. I'm going to America in the summer—I shall be over there some time, I think, and will go on to Europe afterwards. I want to spend some time in

Spain, looking up my mother's family.'

The telephone pealed at this point and Peter rose to answer it. While he was talking, Dan leaned forward and said in a low voice: 'Am I forgiven for my wickedness the other night?'

Cathy smiled. 'Are you truly repentant?' she asked lightly.

He chuckled. 'I should probably repeat the offence if given the chance,' he said.

She ignored this. 'When do you leave for America?' she asked politely.

'About the middle of May,' he said. 'I've been asked to do a lecture tour,' he added, grinning. 'So it seems that my college education is going to stand me in good stead at last. I suppose my title attracts them—they never thought of asking me before although my book sold fairly well in that country.'

She glanced at him quickly. 'Your book? I didn't know you were a writer.'

'I'm not, really,' he replied. 'It was my first and only attempt to break into the literary world—and no one was more surprised than myself when it was an outstanding success.'

'You've not written anything since?'

He shook his head. 'No. I'm too lazy. But I might write another book when I come back from America—my publishers are growing very displeased with me that I haven't yet provided them with a second best-seller. It's two years now since they published my first feeble brainchild.'

She found it easy to talk to him because they were on a safe subject yet all the time she was very conscious that he had confessed to Peter that he loved her. She found herself seeking some sign of his love in his expression, in the dark eyes, sifting his words for some hidden meaning. But Dan was keeping a very strict rein on himself. He had banished that devil which had tormented him so when he met his Cathryn at the ball. He had reminded himself again and again that she was now Peter's wife and presumably happy in her marriage: that there was no hope for the love he bore her and that he had once been quite reconciled to the fact that they could never find happiness together; he had been compelled by his love to see her again before he left London, but he was determined that in no way should he disturb Peter or Cathryn and despite his levity he deeply regretted the incident which had left more than a mark on his cheek.

Thinking of the title he had mentioned, Cathy said: 'I believe the Americans are very partial to titled Englishmen. I wonder if one of their lovely women will capture it for herself.'

He laughed. 'I'm very partial to lovely American women,' he said lightly. 'One never knows—I might return with a Countess despite my determination to remain single all my life.'

Cathy glanced at Peter who was still absorbed in his telephone conversation. From snippets of his remarks, she knew that he was talking to the friend who had entertained them at a night-club on the previous evening.

'I don't think you're the marrying type, Dan,' Cathy said smoothly. 'Too much of a Don Juan!'

He looked down at the glowing end of his cigarette. 'I could reform if necessary, you know,' he said quietly. 'But I've only met one woman who could persuade me it was necessary—and she's quite beyond my touch.'

Cathy frowned slightly. 'Why?'

'Far too good for me,' he said curtly.

It would be too easy to assume that he meant her, Cathy told herself. Peter could have been mistaken in his friend's sincerity. She could not resist saying, without meeting his eyes. 'Surely that would be up to the woman to decide, Dan? Why don't you try your luck?'

He gazed at her until she was forced to look at him, compelled by something more powerful than the desire to avoid his eyes. When their eyes met, he replied: 'It's too late. Some other man tried his luck and won the fair lady—I believe she's very happy with her lot. She would have found me rather a trial as a husband, I'm afraid—so she probably is much better off with the other man.'

A faint flush tinged Cathy's cheeks for now she could not mistake his meaning —not while his eyes burned into hers and he spoke with such fervour.

'You should have given her a chance to decide for herself,' she stumbled through stiff lips.

He shrugged. 'I know myself too well,' he said. 'I have all the assets that fond mothers warn their daughters against and I doubted my ability to reform for any great length of time.'

'Love is a very powerful force,' she murmured.

'But it cannot work miracles,' he returned with a wry smile.

'I think you underestimate your good

qualities,' Cathy told him and her hands tightened on the arm of her chair to quieten their trembling. 'Loving you, I—she ...' the colour surged hotly at the stupid mistake she had made but she went on steadily: 'She would have gladly overlooked your faults.'

He smiled then and it was vibrant with tender warmth and love. He put out a hand to rest it on hers for a brief moment. 'Yes, I believe she would,' he said. 'But I care too much to risk disappointing her—as I said, she has found happiness with this other man and I've no intention of causing any more trouble.'

At this point, Peter replaced the telephone and came back to them. Cathy busied herself with pouring him a fresh cup of tea, hoping that her cheeks had lost their glow and that Peter would not suspect that Dan had caused her to lose her composure.

Some minutes later, Dan rose to his feet and said that he had to be going. Cathy looked up at him and in her eyes was a plea for a last gesture of his love, one last assurance.

Dan bent over her and brushed his lips across her cheek. 'Goodbye, Cathryn,' he said in a low voice. 'Be happy.' Then he turned to Peter and walked out of the lounge with him, leaving Cathy to sit with hands clenched so tightly that her fingernails cut into her palms and a heart too full for tears. Now she knew that Dan loved her as only a man with such depths of passion, such single-minded purpose and such a reckless past can love. She knew that no other woman had ever or would ever be so important to Dan and this was a grain of comfort. She knew also that with his last words he had finally relinquished all claim to her and it was indeed a goodbye.

CHAPTER 11

They did not make the journey to Norfolk and Dan did not press them in his infrequent letters. As it happened, he was very busy with the preparations for his American tour. It was a matter of great importance to him that he should leave the management of the estate in the hands of a trustworthy and reliable agent. He interviewed several likely applicants and eventually decided on an ex-Army officer who had some experience of estate management. The two men formed an instant mutual liking and in the few weeks which lapsed between Captain Hardy's installation and Dan's departure for America a firm friendship developed. Captain Hardy absorbed Dan's instructions intelligently and proved himself capable. So

Dan finally left England at the beginning of May with an easy mind. He carried with him too the definite suspicion that Captain Hardy was smitten with Cleo's charms and he hoped that when he finally returned to England he would find that Cleo had switched her rather obvious affection from himself to the captain.

Cathy's only news of Dan for some time was through the newspapers and one brief letter which he wrote, telling of the warm reception awaiting him in America, the kindness of the American people, his hopes for the success of the tour and a promise to visit them when he was again in England.

Cathy did not forget Dan. He was often in her thoughts but as the months went by her interest turned naturally to the coming child. Not only was there a strong maternal streak in her character but also she clung to the hope that the baby would cement her marriage and finally disperse all her nostalgia and longing for Dan.

She liked living at Chisholm House and the year proved to be a happy one. She found many things to occupy her time and Peter had always been the ideal companion. She led a very active life until the burden of the expected child forced her to take things more easily. She was cosseted and fussed over by both families who were delighted by the prospect of her motherhood. The colonel made no secret of his great pleasure and his conversation turned more and more to the subject of his first grandchild. The Wallis parents had enjoyed the prospect of Graham's child from afar, for Paul had been born in Paris, but the knowledge that Peter's child would be born in the same house as both their sons pleased them both very much. They were very solicitous about Cathy's health and welfare and she bore with all the attentions patiently although she privately thought them a little unnecessary for she held the now old-fashioned view that childbirth was a very natural function and something to be taken in one's stride.

Peter was very happy for he firmly believed that his son—he was convinced that the child would be a boy—would make all the difference to the relationship between himself and his wife. He knew that although Cathy would never entirely free herself from the enchantment of Dan she had now completely reconciled herself to life without him. In time, Peter assured himself, Cathy would realize that only he could have made her so happy: she would instinctively understand that marriage with Dan would have been a failure, remembering his restless nature, his arrogant indifference to convention and his nomadic habits.

With the arrival of his son as the summer was drawing to its close, Peter finally decided that the spectre of Cathy's love for Dan held no more terrors. He knew that it still lived in her heart but believed it had little power to disturb the even tenor of their marriage.

When Cathy held her small son in her arms for the first time, her eyes were shining with happiness. She held him close, cradling him against her breast, studying him with all the intense eagerness of the new mother. He was a sturdy child with strong limbs, a thick down of red-gold curls and bright blue eyes. In the small yet determined features, Cathy fancied a resemblance to Peter and she was content but he was just as certain that their son had inherited his mother's looks.

Cathy quickly recovered and the boy thrived in the country air and on such loving attention. He was a good baby, content to sleep most of his day on the lawn in his pram, and he seemed to understand from the very beginning that nights were precious to those who cared for him. An excellent young nurse was engaged for him but Cathy adored her son and wanted to be his sole attendant. She never tired of gazing at his innocent face and planning his future for him in the age-old tradition of mothers.

To his dismay, Peter found himself to be an unnecessary member of the household. He was pushed into the background more and more, for not only Cathy but the grandparents too were devoted to the child and all their interest was focused on him. It seemed that no other child had ever been so healthy, so handsome, so placid and so intelligent as his son.

They named the boy Andrew Graham. Peter had chosen the names and this was almost the only concession that Cathy made to his claim to paternity. For the rest, he often told himself bitterly that Cathy seemed to imagine Andrew was entirely her own achievement. He was awkward with small babies and often declared that he had no idea which way to hold them. If he picked Andrew up, he would be sure to dissolve into loud cries and then Cathy would hastily rescue her small son, throwing Peter an indignant, reproachful glance. She was so engrossed in the wonder which attached to the miracle of her first-born that she neglected Peter quite unconsciously.

At first, Peter was very patient and told himself with his usual placid philosophy that in time the novelty would wear off and he would regain his sunny, companionable and charming young wife. But the months went by and Cathy was still more mother than wife and Peter began to look for companionship and affection outside his home and family.

He found Diana a friendly companion for she frankly declared her indifference to babies and he could depend on a variety of conversational gambits when he was with her. Peter was suffering from a surfeit of baby talk and although he looked forward to the time when his son would be old enough to be interesting, a companion to him and a willing pupil under his father's guidance, at the moment he had no hand in his son's welfare or early training. He found it difficult to suppress the resentment and jealousy which Andrew aroused in him—a far greater jealousy than he had ever felt when Cathy had openly adored Dan Ritchie. He was helpless to fight his son's influence on Cathy. He could only watch her adoration for Andrew grow daily more complete. Peter could not compete against the innocent, flower-like charms of his son.

Diana welcomed his company for she had always liked Peter. She had matured during the past two years although she was still but eighteen. They rode together, swam together, went fishing and shooting, walking or driving. He played billiards with the colonel and occasionally escorted Bess and Diana to cocktail parties, dances or picnics.

He sometimes felt a little guilty that he should enjoy the company of the two young girls so much but he reminded himself that Cathy smiled benevolently upon the circumstance and always refused any invitation to accompany them. She usually looked reproachful and said that Andrew might need her. It was useless to reply that they employed a very capable nurse to care for their son for it was obvious that Cathy trusted no one but herself with Andrew's welfare.

It soon became generally known that Peter Wallis was always available to make up a party for dinner or the theatre or shooting or hunting and he was much in demand for he had always been a popular young man. Rumours flew about the county that he and his wife were drifting apart despite the recent birth of their son, but none of these rumours came to the ears of those concerned and Cathy continued to put Andrew before her husband in all things and at all times.

She was quite unconscious of the effect her reaction to motherhood had on Peter. She sincerely believed that her first duty was to Andrew while he was so little and helpless. She had no realization that the son they had both wanted so much was proving to be a wedge which increasingly forced them apart rather than the welcome cementing of their marriage. Andrew had taken the place of Dan in her life for she lavished all her adoration, all her generous and impulsive warmth and all her vital interest on him. While she had her son, nothing else mattered.

When Peter sought her embraces, driven by the urgency of his love for her which could never change despite the coldness she showed him, she was generous to him, and kind, but her response was dutiful rather than loving and he felt that he held a stranger in his arms. Hurt and rebuffed, passion began to die in him and by the time Andrew was ten months old, their life together consisted of nothing but the fact of marriage and their mutual parentage of Andrew.

Everyone but Cathy noticed the change in him. A few lines were etched about his mouth and eyes where before had been serenity. Sometimes an unexpected glance would surprise a hint of sadness in his once laughing blue eyes. His natural gaiety was a little subdued and his enjoyment of life seemed to be forced on occasions. His parents worried but said nothing for they had seldom interfered in their sons' lives and they were confident of his ability to sort things out for himself. The colonel, who doted on his grandson and was far too proud of Cathy to listen to a word of criticism of her, took the line that Peter was to blame for the rift in his marriage which was obvious to all but Cathy. Lorna Ames was the only one to make up her mind to talk to Peter and try to help him. She was very fond of Peter and it grieved her to notice his unhappiness. Shrewdly, she had observed from the beginning Cathy's obsession with Andrew and had known what the outcome must be unless she came to her senses and realized that she had a husband as well as a child. Lorna had experienced this same situation before with her own parents when a son had been born late in life to them when she had been in her early teens. She had been old enough to understand and sympathize with both parents but too young to offer advice. Now she was in a position to help Peter and she was determined to do it. But it was not enough to talk to Peter: she must eventually tackle Cathy too and endeavour to make her realize that her attitude was destroying her marriage which had seemed so happy until Andrew's birth.

It was not difficult to draw Peter's confidence. He had kept things to himself for so long, brooding over the rift which seemed to have crept into his marriage, blaming his son rather than his wife because he loved her, and Lorna's sympathetic ear was offered at the right time. He found himself openly telling her of the difficulties between Cathy and he without barely knowing how the subject had arisen.

'I don't think she really loves me any

the less,' he said slowly, standing with his back to the hearth, his hands thrust deep into his pockets. A slight frown marred his pleasant countenance and his blue eyes were troubled. 'But she seems to forget that she has a husband as well as a child. Yet I don't think she deliberately neglects me.' He sighed. 'She's a different person since Andrew was born.'

Lorna nodded, her firm hands which had so often quietened a rebellious horse now busy with the coffee-pot and the exquisite china. The fragrance of hot, steaming coffee rose into her room. She wore a light tweed suit and her short dark hair was swept back from the intelligent forehead. Grey-blue eyes smiled sympathetically at him from the tanned, attractive face and he was strongly reminded at that moment of Diana who so resembled her mother.

'You haven't talked this over with Cathy herself?'

He shook his head. 'No. We used to be able to thrash out any problems sensibly but this is different. I think she resents criticism these days. Besides, as I told you, I'm sure she doesn't even know what she's doing to us. If I accused her of putting Andrew before me, she'd probably be amazed and incredulous.' He moved to take the cup she offered him and then stood, stirring the spoon round and round in the coffee unconsciously.

'You know, Peter, Cathy's reaction to becoming a mother is quite a common thing,' Lorna said slowly. 'Many women push their husbands into the background at such a time.'

Peter shrugged. 'I know that. But does it usually last so long? After all, the boy is ten months old!'

Lorna looked up at him, her eyes enigmatic. She had not missed the faint resentment in his tone when he mentioned his son. Then she said: 'How were things between you before he was born? You seemed very happy—were you?'

'Why do you ask that?' he asked quickly.

'What possible bearing could our previous happiness have on the present state of affairs?'

'I'm no psychologist,' she replied evenly, 'but I think Cathy has deliberately made Andrew the centre of her interest, the focal point of her life. If she had been disappointed in her marriage or unhappy with you, Peter, this would be a fairly normal reaction. Children are a great comfort to a woman who is disillusioned in marriage—they don't begin to disappoint one until they're much older, as a rule.'

Peter drained his coffee. 'We've always been very happy,' he said firmly. There was a trace of stubborn pride in his voice. 'Until now,' he added bitterly.

Lorna took a cigarette. 'I think someone should talk seriously to Cathy,' she said casually. 'She's very naughty to let your marriage break up in this way.'

'It isn't Cathy's fault!' he said sharply.

Lorna raised her eyebrows. 'The on-looker sees most of the game, Peter,' she reminded him, 'and I think Cathy is entirely to blame.'

He shook his head stubbornly. 'No. I can't blame Cathy.'

'Then who would you blame?' Lorna asked, intently studying the glowing end of her cigarette.

He gave a dry laugh. 'That's a poser, isn't it? I could say myself. After all, I'm the boy's father ...'

Lorna interrupted him: 'But in fact you blame Andrew for coming between you, don't you?'

He looked at her sharply. 'He's only a baby—that's ridiculous!'

She was silent for a moment, thinking. Peter was not wholly without love for his son, that was obvious. A little of his jealousy was directed against Cathy for denying him all contact with Andrew: some against the child for taking Cathy away from him.

Before she could speak, Peter added, flushing a little: 'Yes, you're right. I do blame Andrew and I know it's most unfair. But how the devil can I hope to compete with my own son? I'm so damn unimportant to Cathy these days!'

'Would you like me to talk to Cathy?' Lorna asked quietly. 'We've always been the best of friends—she's just like my own daughter. I don't think she'd resent interference from me.'

'I'm sure she wouldn't,' Peter said eagerly. 'I know she'd listen to you—I wish you would talk things over with her.'

'I might say all the wrong things,' Lorna warned him with a smile.

He ran his hand over his fair hair. 'Say anything you like—but let's have an end to this ridiculous coldness between Cathy and myself! I can't stand much more of it—believe me I can't Lorna! I shall take myself off to the Azores or somewhere, and leave Cathy to her mother instinct!' He sounded so wild and distraught that Lorna repressed the smile which flickered in her eyes and touched his arm with a sympathetic hand.

'I'll do my best, Peter,' she promised. 'I'll talk to Cathy at my earliest opportunity—although I feel that you would be the best person to discuss this with her.'

'I can't do that,' he said unhappily. 'I've tried so many times but she's always so full of Andrew and his latest achievement!'

When he had gone, Lorna sat for a long time over fresh coffee, thinking about her promise and worrying about Peter, for she really believed that he could not go on much longer as things were. She would be extremely sorry to see that marriage break up but she could not deny that it might come to this in the end. She sighed. A child should be a blessing to both parents and it invariably brought its own welcome and love. It was apparent that Peter loved Andrew but he was scarcely allowed any demonstration of his affection—it was not surprising that resentment should be forcing out love.

Diana came hurrying into the room by

way of the french windows. She was quick to sense her mother's unusual soberness. 'Is anything wrong, Mother?' she asked swiftly.

Lorna smiled absently at her youngest daughter. 'No, my dear. I'm merely having a quiet think.'

'I've just seen Peter striding over the park,' Diana said slowly. 'I waved to him but he didn't appear to see me. He looked like a thundercloud—did you upset him?' Her tone was lightly accusing.

Lorna raised her eyebrows. 'Good heavens, no! We've just had coffee together ...'

'Then you've been talking about Cathy,' Diana said shrewdly. 'She makes me furious, Mother, the way she treats Peter. Why can't she appreciate him for the good husband he is? I bet there aren't many men who'd stand for her continual drooling about Andrew!'

'It isn't our business, Diana,' Lorna reproved.

'Then why have you been discussing it

with Peter?' her daughter replied swiftly.

'I didn't say we had been talking about Cathy,' Lorna reminded her.

'No, but you didn't say it immediately so don't prevaricate now, Mother. Honestly, my blood boils sometimes—I'd like to give her a piece of my mind ...'

'You'll do no such thing,' Lorna said sharply.

Diana tossed her dark head rebelliously. There were times when not even her mother could control the wilful streak which ran through her nature. 'Won't I?' she demanded. 'It's time that someone made her see sense.' Her quick temper was aroused. She was devoted to Peter and only the fear of incurring his displeasure had prevented her from speaking her mind to Cathy.

'I forbid you to interfere, Diana!' There was a warning note in Lorna's voice which usually quelled her children.

But Diana was seeing too vividly the expression in Peter's face a few minutes ago, the despondent poise of his head, the unhappiness which had been apparent in his carriage and she longed to fly to his defence. Assuming an obedient air she said: 'Very well, Mother.' She accepted some coffee and they talked of other things while she drank it, but all the while her mind was recalling the many incidents she had noticed, the many times when Cathy's attitude to Peter had made her fume. As soon as she could, she rose to her feet and said casually: 'Peter promised to take me to the Tarn this afternoon. I think I'll go seek him.' She made her escape and hurried over to Chisholm House. It was true that they had made arrangements to drive to a local beauty spot where they could swim in the cool, famous lake but she was determined to tell Cathy a few home truths while her anger was still hot.

CHAPTER 12

Cathy was playing with her son on the
terrace. It was an attractive picture, for
the sun gleamed on the rich auburn of
Cathy's hair and reflected its rays in the
red-gold curls of her son. He gurgled with
laughter as she held him high in the air
and then brought him down again with a
rush. Her face was alight with love and
happiness and suddenly she caught him
close to her breast and buried her lips in
the soft, cuddly folds of his neck.

Diana walked slowly up the stone steps
and approached them. Her temper had
cooled down a little during the swift walk
across the park towards Chisholm House,
but her determination was still strong.

Cathy heard her footsteps and turned.
'Hallo, Diana,' she greeted her. 'Have

you come in search of Peter? He's just gone up to change.' She held the child towards Diana. 'Isn't he beautiful?' she asked rapturously.

Diana backed away. 'Don't give him to me,' she said swiftly. 'I shall drop him.'

Cathy laughed. 'You sound like Peter.'

'I sympathize with Peter,' Diana said quickly. 'I know just how he feels. Babies are terrifying unless one has had a lot to do with them.'

There was something in her tone that gave Cathy pause. She looked up at Diana, her brow creasing slightly. 'Peter's had ten months to learn how to hold a baby,' she said slowly. 'He's just not interested.'

'You've never given him the chance,' Diana told her abruptly. 'You make it very obvious that Andrew is your sole property. I wonder that you don't hang a *Keep Off* sign about his neck.'

Cathy was puzzled by this attack but she laughed lightly. 'Perhaps I am a little possessive,' she admitted easily. 'But he's such a darling.' She decided to change the subject. 'Where are you going, Diana? Somewhere nice?'

'The Tarn. Why don't you come with us, Cathy?'

'Oh, I couldn't. It's Isobel's day off and I ...'

'Can't leave Andrew,' Diana finished for her. A note of utter boredom crept into her voice. 'That's always your cry, Cathy. You know very well that Mrs Wallis would gladly take care of Andrew for a few hours but you won't give him up to anyone. Is it any wonder that Peter has to find enjoyment with other people? You're less than a wife to him since Andrew became so important.'

Sensing the atmosphere, the child began to cry and hastily Cathy hushed him, holding him close. She rose to her feet and began to pace the terrace, hurt by Diana's accusation and bewildered by the girl's evident anger against her.

'I don't understand you, Diana,' she said

at last as Andrew's cries quietened.

'That's because you don't wish to understand,' Diana snapped. 'Andrew is the be-all and end-all of your existence and it's driving Peter further and further away from you. Do you understand that? All the county is talking about you and Peter—I've heard gossip which I've kept from Peter because it would only make him unhappier than you do by neglecting him for Andrew.'

Cathy stopped pacing. The colour drained from her face and her green eyes seemed to blaze against the sudden pallor. She laid Andrew down in his pram and carefully covered him up. Then she turned to Diana. 'What gossip?'

Diana shrugged. 'I don't see why you shouldn't know what people are saying about you. They say that your marriage is on the rocks, that you never cared for Peter—that you only married him because someone else let you down. They also say that Andrew isn't his child and that's why you've drifted apart since he was born.'

'That isn't true!' Cathy said slowly, catching her breath. 'How dare people say such lies! None of it is true!'

'None of it?' queried Diana meaningly. 'Then you don't think that you and Peter are breaking up.'

'No. Why should we? We're perfectly happy ...'

Diana let out an exasperated sigh. 'You are—wrapped up in that baby! It's incredible—but you really have been blind to Peter's need of you as a wife. I began to wonder if you were deliberately using Andrew to make him unhappy but now I see that you've merely been blind. Well, it's time that someone told you the truth, Cathy, so I will. If you don't snap out of this obsession for Andrew and give your husband a little of your time and attention, I warn you that one day you'll be without a husband. I wonder how much comfort you'll find in Andrew then!'

Cathy listened to this tirade in absolute

silence and amazement. Then she turned to lean against the balustrade and looked out over the gardens. Diana's words had been a great shock to her. She had not known that Peter was unhappy. He had never mentioned that he resented Andrew taking up so much of her time. Did he think her love for the child was an obsession too? Had he heard any of the rumours which were running around the county? Why had he never told her he was unhappy? Her thoughts ran amok but through them all ran the vein of truth as she realized that she had indeed neglected Peter. She racked her memory to recall the last time they had gone anywhere together, the last time she had been absolutely alone with him, the last time they had talked together without any mention of Andrew, the last time Peter had come to her room at night with love in his eyes and endearments on his lips. Her life seemed to have only revolved around Andrew of late and it was all too obvious now that

Peter had been pushed more and more out of her life. Tears sprang to her eyes and she did not resent Diana's crude attack for she was glad to know the truth at last.

'I didn't know—I had no idea ...' she stumbled and she turned to Diana with sincerity in her eyes.

'That's the only extenuating circumstance,' Diana said harshly. 'None of us could believe that you would have let things go so far if you knew what was happening—but you should have known, Cathy. After all, Peter is your husband and one supposes that you love him—unless there is more than a grain of truth in all the rumours?'

'That's quite enough, Diana!' Peter said sharply from the windows that led into the lounge. 'I think you've said all that's necessary.' His eyes were blazing with anger and the girl quailed beneath his glance.

She said with quick defence of her actions: 'Well, it was time she knew! No one else would tell her—not even you!'

Cathy turned towards Peter and in her eyes was a plea for forgiveness, for understanding. He walked slowly across the terrace to her side. 'I hope you didn't pay any attention to that pack of nonsense,' he said easily.

'It wasn't nonsense,' Cathy replied. 'It was the truth and she's quite right. It was time I knew—and I wish you had told me, Peter.' She was still stunned by realization but she spoke bravely enough and the smile she gave Diana was a grateful, affectionate one.

'Fools rush in!' commented Peter dryly with a glance at Diana which still held a trace of anger. The girl flushed.

'That's unkind!' Cathy said quickly. 'Diana was only trying to help and I for one appreciate her motives.'

'I'm told the way to hell is paved with good intentions,' Diana put in lightly. 'I can understand why. I'm sorry if you're annoyed, Peter, but I really thought the thing had gone far enough. You weren't prepared to thrash it out with Cathy and although everyone else knew what was happening, no one would intervene. Well, the truth's out now so let's hope there'll be a few changes at Chisholm House in the near future.' She turned to leave them. 'I guess we won't be going to the Tarn today, after all—I'll see you later.'

They watched Diana walk purposefully across the park, head held high, her firm young body erect, strength of character in every line. Then Peter turned to Cathy.

'I could wring her neck,' he said without venom. 'But I knew she'd let fly one day—it's been brewing up with her for weeks.'

'And with you too?' Cathy asked slowly.

'Longer than that,' he replied curtly, not meeting her eyes.

She put her hand on his arm. 'Peter, why didn't you tell me? Why did you let me go on neglecting you when a few words would have made all the difference?'

He shrugged. 'Pride, I suppose. And the fear that you would think me petty and unreasonable. I just kept hoping that one day you would once again be the Cathy I married instead of merely the mother of our son.'

At mention of the child, she glanced at the pram and bent over the sleeping baby to adjust his clothing. The gesture was automatic and casual and she instantly turned away again, turned back to Peter who stood watching her. She smiled at him warmly and moved closer to him, putting her arms around him. The impulsive gesture touched his heart and broke down the barrier he had erected in self-defence. He drew her close and touched her rich hair with his lips.

'I'm sorry, Peter,' she murmured. 'I didn't intend to hurt you, to make you unhappy.'

'I know,' he assured her. 'Let's forget it all now, darling. I don't want you to neglect Andrew for me—I know you wouldn't anyway and I don't expect it. All I ask is that you share him with me and remember that there are many times when I want your company.'

She hugged him. 'I'll try to remember that there are other subjects of conversation besides babies, too, Peter.'

Cathy kept her word. Now that Diana's words had shaken her out of her rut, she kept remembering how often she had refused Peter's company and how patient he had been with her during the recent months. She realized that she had indeed been obsessed by Andrew and that no baby needed the amount of loving attention that she had drawn about him like a shawl. She forced herself to relinquish him to the care of his nurse: she allowed her mother-in-law to take care of him at times so that she and Peter could go out together; in short, she relegated her son to the proper perspective and concentrated on being a wife to Peter once again. It was not as difficult as at first it seemed for he helped her in many ways and once she had left Andrew for an afternoon with Isobel and driven to the Tarn with Peter, her first step towards regaining the old comfortable companionship, it became much easier to assure herself that the boy was perfectly safe and contented without her. The first afternoon was an anxious one, but she was determined to hide her worries, silly though most of them were, and it was a great relief when they returned to Chisholm House to find that nothing dire had happened in her absence. She and Peter were both much happier for he filled a need in her life that she had forgotten existed since Andrew's birth and he was delighted that Diana's impetuous words had done nothing but good.

Lorna was annoyed at first to hear that Diana had deliberately defied her but her annoyance faded when she discovered that all was now well between Peter and Cathy. It took a little time naturally for the bonds of motherhood were very firm, but Peter had a vast fund of patience and the knowledge that Cathy was doing her best to re-adjust their life together.

Sometimes Cathy tried to delve into her inner self to discover why Andrew had been so vitally important to her. She had clung to him as though he was a lifeline. Was it a desperate need to erase the longing for Dan that she had used Andrew as a substitute for the great love within her? This could be the answer, she knew, for during the first months of Andrew's life, Dan's memory had faded and she had been able to think of him without the old ache in her heart. Since she had released her hold on her son, trying to fight down the possessiveness he aroused in her, her thoughts had turned again to Dan and she often wondered about him: how he was, if he were still in America, when she would see him again, if he still cared for her or whether he had found consolation elsewhere, how she would react when he finally returned to England and came to

Buckhurst to see them as he had promised? So many questions and she knew none of the answers. The only thing she was sure of was that his name still had the power to make her heart leap and the blood surge through her veins. She could call his face to memory and the dear, handsome lineage touched the secret compartment of her heart where her love still lingered. She would admit this to herself and then hastily push away the memory of him, almost wishing that they might never meet again and yet knowing that it was her dearest wish to see him once more.

He had written congratulating them on the birth of their son and promised to stand as sponsor at his christening. He had told them that he was still not sure when he would be in England again as he was then leaving shortly for the Continent. His letter had been brief and formal as Cathy's reply, but she knew they could rely on his promise and refused to have the boy christened until Dan could be present at the ceremony. Peter suggested that someone could stand proxy for Dan but Cathy had set her heart on having Dan present and nothing would sway her. It was an unimportant matter, Peter decided, and did not press it. But he too wondered how much longer it would be before his friend came back to England. Dan had been often abroad but never for such a long spell and Peter remarked once to Cathy that Dan must have the greatest confidence in the agent he had appointed to the estate else he would have been home long before.

When Dan did return it was with typical suddenness. Peter was in the library writing letters when the door opened and Dan walked in, tall, very tanned, a warm smile illuminating his handsome face. Peter looked up, expecting Cathy and the surprise was evident in his eyes. A brief moment, then he was on his feet with hand outstretched.

'Dan! Where did you spring from? When did you get back?'

The two men shook hands. 'I've been over here a week,' Dan replied. 'Hardy had a stupid accident with a gun and they sent for me.'

Peter poured a drink for himself and his friend. 'It's grand to see you after all this time. Cathy and I thought you'd decided to settle abroad.'

Dan grinned. 'It's been a long time,' he admitted. 'But I've had some good experiences and, my publishers will be pleased to hear, I've brought back two manuscripts with me.' He added easily: 'How is Cathryn?'

'She's fine! And our son and heir is a strapping youngster—wait until you see him!'

Dan nodded. 'Perhaps we'll get around to his christening now I'm home,' he said.

'Tell me about Hardy?' Peter demanded. 'Did you say he'd had a shooting accident?'

'Yes. Shot himself in the foot. Very nasty and they had to amputate, I'm afraid. He's such a grand chap—it's a great pity. It'll be some time before he's fit enough to come back, so it looks like I'm grounded for a while.' Dan drained his drink and frowned over it as he thought about the energetic and likeable Captain Hardy. He went on to enlarge on the accident and Peter listened intently. Then Dan said idly: 'By the way, Cleo Vanney's engaged to him. They were planning to get married next month so this is all rather a blow. She's still determined to marry him—thinks the world of him and doesn't turn a hair when he says he hasn't any intention of letting her marry a cripple. They'll fix him up all right with an artificial foot and in time no one will know the difference. I admire Cleo very much for standing by him.'

Peter grinned. 'So her father's wishes have been disappointed?'

'Afraid so. She'll have to be content with a captain for a husband instead of an earl—Cleo isn't worried and doesn't give a damn for her father's opinion.' He looked about him. 'By the way, where is Cathryn?'

'Probably romping with Andrew in the nursery. I'll go and tell her you're here—she'll be thrilled to death!' He went towards the door.

Dan stopped him: 'Are you two happy?' he asked slowly.

Peter turned with his hand on the door handle. 'Yes,' he replied firmly. 'We've had a few difficulties but they have all been straightened out now. Our marriage seems to be quite a success—of course, Andrew helps, you know.'

Dan nodded. 'I envy you,' he said abruptly. 'A wife and a son—I should have the same. I wish now that I'd married years ago. It's a good thing to have some family ties.'

Peter laughed and said, teasing him: 'You're growing old, man. Years ago the very thought of marriage made you shudder.'

Dan laughed his agreement. 'It still

would if there was any chance of it, I expect. I'm glad I got Cleo off my back at last, anyway—and she couldn't have picked a nicer fellow than Hardy. I'd make a devil of a husband for any woman—better to stay single.'

'I won't be long,' Peter assured him. 'Pour yourself another drink. I'll bring Cathy down with me.'

The door closed behind him and Dan sat very still for a moment, gazing at the wooden panels. He was tense, eager and expectant. During the drive from Norfolk he had whiled the time with thoughts of Cathryn, of her reaction to his unexpected arrival, of her present emotions where he was concerned. She was happy. Peter had sounded very sure. She had a son and this surely made for a successful marriage. So long since he had seen her and during his travels her memory had been his constant companion. He was a very lonely man despite the crowds which surrounded him, the many friends he had made, the many women who had made no secret of their warm feeling for him. No woman had moved him and he had not felt the need of solace. It had become a habit to take the memory of Cathryn with him wherever he went: he liked to recall their first meeting and the swiftness of falling in love, the meetings which had followed—so few and so cherished; he needed no photographs of her for her lovely face crowned with the glory of her auburn hair was indelibly imprinted on his memory. His love for Cathryn was the one vital part of the man these days. It amused him to hear himself spoken of as a reformed rake: he smiled when his friends said that he was no longer an exciting, reckless devil; his smile grew even broader when he was asked if some woman had changed him so much. His answers were always swift and skilfully cynical, razor-sharp and to the point. The truth was that his days of light loving, gambling and drinking, exchanging risqué stories and throwing wild parties were over. He found no pleasure in his former pursuits. They were dull and tasteless and insipid to him now. He longed only for the sweetness of forbidden fruit—the love and the warmth of another man's wife. This love he knew for Cathryn was eternal and unchangeable and he wanted it no other way. It might avail him nothing—no, he knew it would always be in vain—but he had chosen the path he walked alone and he would not turn back. Cathryn was beyond his grasp but at least he could love from afar and hope for her happiness.

He rose and poured himself another drink. He jerked his head back and the liquid seared his throat. He was trembling, nervous as a boy, a tautness in his stomach and the blood running like fire through his veins.

Cathryn's lovely face was suddenly before his eyes and it bore the appealing, pleading, warm expression that he had seen at their last meeting—the appeal of beauty, the plea for some sign of his love, the warmth of her love for him. He murmured her name aloud and then shook his head like a swimmer coming from the water as though to clear his brain of the intoxication that was the woman he loved.

He stiffened and braced himself as he heard footsteps in the hall. Pride reared his head and he drew himself to his full height. He composed his features and waited, turned towards the door, his eyes on the wooden panels, waiting for the first glimpse of the woman he had not seen for so long yet whose beauty and sweetness always lived with him.

CHAPTER 13

The swift colour flooded Cathy's cheeks and her eyes were suddenly joyous. 'Dan? Here?' she asked with a note of incredulity in her voice.

Peter was too pleased and excited on his own account to notice the flutter of excitement, the tumult which betrayed itself by the colour, the bright eyes and the quick catch of her breath. 'Yes. Isn't it just like him to descend upon us without a word of warning?' Peter laughed. 'I told him I'd take you straight down to meet him—are you ready?'

Cathy's hands went to her neat shining hair and then she hurried to a mirror to study her reflection. 'Lord! I'm a mess!' she declared in horror.

Peter came behind her and put his arms

around her tenderly. 'You're absolutely beautiful!' he assured her and kissed her neck. She turned her head to smile into his eyes. 'Anyway, there isn't time to powder your nose or anything. I don't want to leave Dan on his own—he'll empty the decanter if I don't hurry back.' His grin belied the words.

Cathy's heart was thudding in her throat and her hands were suddenly damp. She admonished herself sternly not to be a fool, to remember that she was Peter's wife and the mother of his son, to hide this ridiculous tumult of emotion and greet Dan merely as the good friend that he was to them both.

She hurried across to the play-pen and lifted her son into her arms. 'He'll want to see Andrew,' she said quickly. 'Let's take him down with us, Peter.' It was a defence against Dan's attractions, against the surging, leaping love in her breast. Meet him as the mother of this handsome, curly-haired child of a successful marriage:

thrust him away from her instinctive heart; prove to him that he meant nothing after all this time.

Peter looked at her curiously. Then he nodded. 'If you like,' he agreed. 'But wouldn't you like to talk to Dan before introducing him to his godson?' He added lightly: 'Dan's never seen you with a baby in your arms—won't it be a shock to him?'

Cathy busied herself with brushing the red-gold curls from Andrew's forehead and buttoning his playsuit more firmly. 'Why should it?' she asked indifferently. 'He knows we have a child. Besides, Andrew wants to meet his Uncle Dan, don't you darling?'

If Peter knew that his wife was using Andrew as a barrier, a refuge, a proof against her old love for Dan, he made no sign. He was very anxious to observe their reaction to each other. He wanted to know if Dan still cared for Cathy—more important, he wanted to know if Cathy still cared for Dan. He did not stop to think what could be done about it, if anything, if they did still care for each other. He simply wanted the reassurance that the time which had elapsed had been sufficient to erase the love for Dan from Cathy's memory. He wanted to be convinced that she had found enough happiness in their marriage for love to grow in her heart for him. He wanted to be sure that she no longer wanted Dan, either consciously or unconsciously. He had felt reasonably certain that their first sight of each other would tell him one way or the other how things were between them. But she had neatly circumvented his hopes by clasping Andrew to her breast and adopting a maternal expression. It was unlikely that either would betray their real feelings in such a circumstance and he felt a disappointment, a prickle of annoyance. But he said nothing, merely opening the door of the nursery and ushering Cathy from the room.

'How does he look?' Cathy asked as they

went down the wide staircase.

'Very well. Fit and more bronzed than ever—older, of course.' Peter added slyly: 'He seems to have aged more than one would expect from only two years abroad —the beginning of the settling down process.'

Cathy threw him a laughing glance. 'Dan? Settle down? I wouldn't believe it of him!'

The blood pounded in her ears as Peter stepped forward to open the library door and for a moment her senses seemed to swim. Then she pulled herself together and entered the room with a smile.

Dan was facing the door and his eyes were expectant. They exchanged glances and there was a brief, pregnant silence. Then Dan moved forward, completely master of himself now.

'So this is the young rascal who's taken my place in your affections?' he demanded and he took Andrew from her arms, swinging him high. 'Hallo, young man,' he said, laughing up at the boy. 'You're certainly a credit to your parents, aren't you? Bonny and good-looking—strong too,' he added as Andrew struggled in his hold.

'He doesn't take kindly to strangers,' Cathy told him, glad of the child's presence to ease the atmosphere.

Dan lowered him and Andrew pummelled his chest in his struggles to escape from the big, powerful, dark man. Dan laughed and put him down on the thick carpet. Then he turned to Cathy and took her hands. 'How well you look,' he approved. 'And this new mature look—it's most becoming, Cathryn.'

She smiled up at him. 'Thank you, Dan. You're looking very well yourself.' She was very composed now and her heart had ceased trying to fly out of her breast. She appraised him eagerly, noticing the deep tan, the new air about him which accounted for Peter's remark of age. She did not miss the new lines which were etched about the mouth and eyes, the slight, distinguished whiteness about his temples, the look in his dark eyes which spoke of loneliness and longing and her sympathy went out to him.

She went to sit down in a comfortable chair and Dan perched on the edge of the desk, swinging his long legs, a cigarette between his lean fingers. Peter moved to the decanter and began to pour drinks. Andrew was investigating the soft pile of the carpet and was perfectly happy now that he was left alone to amuse himself. The big man had frightened him a little and he kept well away from the desk, occasionally glancing towards him with big blue eyes with a wariness that spoke of his fear that he would again be swung up by those powerful arms and dangled above that dark, almost fierce head.

Peter's first garbled description of Dan's arrival had included his reasons for his return and she asked him now about Captain Hardy. He told her quickly, concisely, and she nodded, expressing her regret for the accident but adding that she was glad it had brought him back to England for it was such a long time since they had seen him.

He smiled. 'Seems longer than it actually is for me,' he said. 'But that's because I've done so much in the time. Life hasn't been exactly static for you, either—producing that bonny lad there and now look at the size of him!'

'Quite the best achievement of my life, eh, Dan?' Peter said lightly.

'I don't give you all the credit!' he retorted. 'Looks to me as though the boy strongly resembles his mother. He'll be the rage of the county when he's older with those looks.'

Cathy laughed. 'Don't wish his life away, Dan—or ours either. I want to enjoy his childhood—it'll worry me to death if he is the rage of the county.'

'Nonsense!' he rallied. 'You'll be immensely proud of him—and so shall I.

After all, he's my godson …'

'When we get around to the christening,' Cathy reminded him with a reproachful smile.

'I'm sorry about that. I thought about flying over before I went to Spain—but other things cropped up.'

'Other women, do you mean?' teased Peter, offering him a cigarette. Dan shook his head both to the cigarette and the question.

'No. As a matter of fact, I've disappointed all my friends by reforming. I never look at women these days. I find they bore me—it's a pity for when I see you and Cathryn so happily married and look at the obvious results of that marriage—' with a meaning glance at Andrew—'then I turn my thoughts seriously to trying it for myself.'

A throb of fear startled Cathy and she chided herself swiftly. She was married and out of his reach so why could she blame him if he turned to another woman.

She asked, striving to keep her voice even: 'Don't tell me you're thinking of making Cleo Vanney the happiest woman in the world?'

'Didn't Peter tell you? She's going to marry Captain Hardy—damn fine choice, in my opinion. He'll tame her if no one else can.'

She was pleasantly surprised. 'I hadn't read of the engagement,' she said.

'I believe it was in the papers,' he replied indifferently. 'I didn't see it so I had quite a shock myself. Tell me about your sisters? Any attachments there yet?'

'No,' Cathy replied with a smile. 'I think my father is beginning to despair—Bess seems to care for the ineligible, hard-up types. At the moment, she's madly in love with a Cambridge undergraduate—but she's madly in love with a different man every time we see her. She's living in London now with a girl-friend—wants to assert her independence, so she says.'

Peter put in: 'Wants to have a good time

275

without parents keeping an eagle eye on her, you mean.'

'And the other one—Diana? She was hardly out of the schoolgirl stage when I last saw her.'

Peter answered this question with enthusiasm. 'She's a stunner! Good looks, poise—a real sport, too. She's game for anything—takes after her mother. Wilful little devil with a hot temper but generous and vital and extremely mature for her age.'

Dan raised his eyebrows with a grin. 'Quite taken with your sister, isn't he, Cathy? Don't you ever get jealous?'

Cathy laughed. 'Good heavens no! They're very good friends—they always have been—but she's still a child.'

Dan turned to Peter. 'Where are your parents? Not away, I hope? They were the last time I was here and I was sorry to miss them.'

'Oh, they're around somewhere.' Peter gave a vague gesture.

With a wifely smile at Peter, Cathy said lightly: 'Your mother is lunching with Lady Ayres and your father has gone to Town to see his lawyer.'

'Oh yes, that's right,' Peter agreed. 'They'll be back later. You do intend to stay with us a few days, Dan? We don't mean to let you run out on us after all this time.'

Dan grinned. 'I brought a case with me—so I was rather banking on an invitation.' He indicated Andrew with a gesture of his head. 'I'd like to make friends with that little imp, anyway—a couple of days should be enough to reassure him that I'm a friend of his!'

Later that night, with Dan installed in one of the guest rooms along the corridor, Cathy sat before her dressing-table, brushing her hair and dwelling on the joy of having him near to her even though her love must be denied. Her eyes were bright as emeralds in the clear pure pallor of the camellia-like face and the long, silken tresses fell to her shoulders in a cascade of rich colour enhanced by the soft lighting.

She drew the brush idly through her hair while her thoughts were with Dan in his room three doors away. She was thinking of the change in him which was vastly apparent to one who had loved him for so long and treasured the memory of his dear face. Tears suddenly touched her lashes as she recalled the haunting air of loneliness and inner sadness he carried with him. Why had an unkind Fate decreed that they should love each other and yet be denied happiness together? Why had she rushed into marriage with Peter knowing that she did not and could not love him? Why was it that his offer of freedom and the joyous discovery that Dan returned her love had come at a time when she was in no position to break up their marriage?

Her hand was stilled and she laid down her hairbrush as a sudden thought came to her. Would she have accepted his offer if she had not been carrying Peter's child under her heart? She had never asked herself this before and it suddenly seemed vital to know what her answer must be.

Peter offered her security, the familiarity of old friendship and a loyal love and understanding, ties which would have been very welcome if she had not met and loved Dan. Would she have willingly given up all this to fly into Dan's arms, unknowing of what the future might bring, uncertain of lasting happiness—even unsure of the strength and loyalty of his love? Would her love have been strong enough to stand the tests and trials which marriage with Dan would have thrust upon her?

She had no illusions about Dan—she knew he was restless and unconventional, wild and reckless, a gamester and a rake. He seemed to be a different man now but the vain love and longing for a woman beyond his reach could have done that to him—loneliness and pain could have changed his ways. But would marriage have had the same effect? If she had married him would his first determination to prove himself worthy of her have faded in time? Would she have fought a losing battle against his lifelong habits, his dislike of irksome ties, his lack of convention, his need of freedom? It was not only possible, Cathy told herself firmly—it was more than probable. A man does not alter his ways on marriage. He is likely to resent a wife's attempts to change him and contrarily defy them. A woman has to accept her husband for what he is on the day she marries him. Dan was a man like any other—perhaps more of a man than most and Cathy admitted to herself now in the honesty of her private thoughts that she was not the woman to bring about changes in Dan. Their temperaments were unsuited. She was more like Peter—placid and patient, easy-going and good-humoured—milk and honey, as someone had once taunted her.

Dan needed a woman to stand up to him, to match fire with fire, tempest with tempest—a woman who was prepared to flout convention with him, to ride with him against the wind, to swim with him against the tide—a woman who cared little for the opinion of others—a woman as wild and turbulent as he, as restless and reckless as he. Cathy was not the woman. Dan loved her still because he had not lived with her but she felt sure in that moment of truth that disillusionment would swiftly follow on the heels of marriage to Dan—disillusionment on both sides. He would hurt her again and again because he would not know that his actions hurt her. She would fail him because she did not know how to support him.

Her instinct had told her that Dan still cared for her although his glances had been guarded and his conversation casual. They had not been alone together since his arrival and nothing had passed between them that could be correctly construed by a keen observer. Yet Cathy knew that his feelings had not changed. Time had intensified them. She knew also that he had deliberately stayed away so long to give her time to forget him, to make a success of her marriage. Well, she had not forgotten him: he had grown dearer to her in his absence; but her marriage certainly seemed to be successful and happy. They had surmounted the obstacle which had been Andrew and she had learned to put husband and child in their right perspectives. They were a happy little group and Cathy could not now imagine her life without Peter and Andrew. But if Peter offered her freedom once more, willing to sacrifice his own happiness and even his marriage for her sake, would she take it? She disliked changes and it would be a great uprooting.

Was it possible that she loved Dan still only because he was an unattainable dream? Had she built him up in her heart and her memory to a height that as a man he could not live up to? Had she endowed him with assets and virtues he did not possess only because she found it impossible to love anyone who did not own them? The long separations had surely helped to foster her dreams of him. If they had met more often and grown to know each other more intimately, might it not have proved that they were mistaken in the love they felt? It was so easy to cherish a dream, to love an ideal, to dwell on an enchantment which had flared into life so quickly and never been allowed to die down because it had been fostered by wishful thinking, hopes and dreams and nostalgic memories.

She buried her chin in her hands and soberly studied her reflection while these thoughts flitted through her brain. She was being completely honest with herself and she was surprised at the truth she was finding deep within her heart. Had she in fact been deceiving herself all this long time with a wrong conception of love?

Love stole into one's heart quietly and unobserved, content to dwell there patiently until it was recognised for the precious and valuable gift that it was. It brought no tumult with it, no heady passion, no intoxicating enchantment but a great sweetness and a quiet warmth, an enveloping peace and joyousness.

A new serenity touched Cathy's face and lips and eyes and she knew that the tumult that had been her wild love for Dan had died within her. She was at peace now and she knew herself. A love that was both a blessing and a joy had taken its place and she was thankful and content that it should be so.

She rose to her feet and slipped out of her dressing-gown. She crept in between the silken sheets of her bed and lay in the darkness, glowing with quiet happiness.

A gentle knock on the door brought a sweet smile to her lips, a smile which lingered even while his mouth was pressed gently on hers and his hands caressed her face and hair with tenderness. She drew him down to her and love flowed from her hands, her lips and the eagerness of her slim body.

She lay in his arms and she was content. He was very quiet and his breath was warm on her brow. She sensed his need of silence and did not interrupt his mood with speech. They communed without words and Cathy prayed that he was conscious of her love. It was impossible at this moment to speak of it so her heart whispered it to him and perhaps his own heart heard and responded.

Soon they slept and the early morning sun, weak though it was at this time of the year, broke in through the window panes to smile upon them, auburn head so close on the pillow to that of the man she loved, a smile upon her lips even in sleep.

He woke first and rose up on his elbow to look down upon her lovely face, innocent in repose, the long lashes sweeping in a dark fan across the camellia-like cheeks, the lips curved sweetly. For a long moment he looked upon her then he sighed. Gently, hoping not to disturb her, he left her side, gathered up his gown and quietly left the room for his own.

The gentle closing of the door disturbed her and she stirred, waking. She was immediately conscious that he had gone and she knew a sense of loss for a brief moment. Then she smiled at her folly. She loved him and so he was always with her.

She reached for her wrap and mules and threw back the covers. She ran to the window and looked over the gardens. Snow had fallen in the night, covering the ground and the trees with white beauty, stark and almost painful in its purity. But the bleak sunshine looked down on her and she raised her face to it happily. She felt that she had never been so happy, wondered if she deserved so much happiness and stifled a feeling of guilt because she was suddenly so careless of everyone's happiness but that of herself and the man she loved.

CHAPTER 14

Cathy went into the lounge with a song in her heart and on her lips. She was looking very lovely this morning for the knowledge of her new found love beautified her and made her radiant. She wore a black wool dress and a simple cross and chain was about her neck to relieve the sombre colour.

Dan looked up from the morning papers. He was sprawled in a comfortable armchair, a cigarette burning in the ashtray beside him, surrounded by newspapers. He was dressed in dark blue slacks and a pale blue shirt, open at the neck. He was magnificent and handsome and, for some unknown reason, Cathy was reminded of something her stepmother had said long ago—'*a fine-looking and well-built animal—a black stallion*'.

'Good morning,' he greeted her.

'Good morning, Dan. Where's Peter? Have you seen him?'

'He went down to the stables with his father, I believe. One of the horses has strained a tendon and he wants to have a look at it.'

Cathy nodded. 'Have you had breakfast yet?' she asked politely.

'Yes, thanks.' He indicated the papers. 'Do you want one of these?' He was unaccountably nervous and at a loss for conversation. The night had been a long one and his sleep had been disturbed by dreams of her. He had lain wakeful in the early hours, thinking of Cathryn and wanting her, longing for some way out of the impasse they found themselves in. He had voluntarily taken himself out of her life and he had never regretted a step more. Rebelliously, he had told himself that they loved each other and were entitled to their happiness. If only there was some way to obtain her freedom—despite his long friendship with Peter he gladly wished him at the bottom of the ocean so that he could claim the woman he loved.

Cathy refused the offer of a newspaper and walked to the window, conscious that his eyes were upon her and wishing now that he had never come back into her life. But would she have reached the conclusion which now made her so happy if she had never seen Dan again? His arrival had sparked off the chain of thought which had brought the truth to light.

He rose and came to stand a little behind her. His nearness confused and disturbed her. He laid a tentative hand on her shoulder. 'Cathryn—I've missed you so much,' he murmured. 'My life has been hell without you—loving, wanting you, never a moment when I haven't thought of you.'

'You shouldn't have come here,' she told him with a break in her voice.

'I had to see you again,' he said with the ache of despair behind the words.

She turned to look at him. 'It wasn't a wise thing to do, Dan.'

His hand tightened on her shoulder. 'Wisdom and I are strangers, my Cathryn—I follow my heart not my head!' He caught her hands and held them close. 'I love you!' he said fiercely. 'I've always loved you. I want you so much, my darling—isn't there some way we can be happy together?'

She shook her head. 'No way at all, Dan. I'm Peter's wife and I love him ...'

He interrupted her. 'A dutiful love—but the love we feel for each other goes much deeper than that! We've a right to our happiness, Cathryn—come away with me! Let me take care of you—I swear we'll be happy, I swear it! God, how I love you! My life is nothing without you—and I won't believe that you can be contented with a milk-and-water existence like this.'

She tried to draw her hands away. 'I'm sorry, Dan—but I don't love you.' Her voice was gentle for she hated to hurt him.

His dark eyes were incredulous. 'Let's have no more pretence,' he begged. 'We've sacrificed enough, Cathryn—there are so many years left and I won't live without you any longer!' His words were wild and reckless, his mood desperate.

She withdrew a hand from his grasp and touched his cheek. She was tender with the memory of the love she had once known and her generous heart was aching for his pain and despair. 'My poor Dan!' she said softly. He turned his lips to her fingers and kissed them.

'Love me, Cathryn,' he said fiercely. 'Let me love you! Come away with me now—we'll go abroad—France, Italy, America—I don't care where it is as long as you're with me. In time we'll be married—I want that, Cathryn. I want to call you my wife.'

'No. No.' The words were forced from her.

Suddenly he pulled her against him, so close that the heavy beating of his heart disturbed her senses. She was conscious of the old magnetism which flowed from him, a faint stirring of the old enchantment, and she resented this for she had conquered it and dispelled it and she wanted no more of it. She struggled in his hold. Then his lips were hot on hers, hot and fierce and passionate, and he strained her slim body ever closer. She was powerless against his strength but she wanted to cry a protest, to wrench herself from his arms, to run away from the primitive, instinctive stirring of her blood. When he raised his head, his eyes were triumphant. 'Now say that you don't love me,' he taunted. 'Now refuse to come away with me—if you can!' He added softly: 'You know that we were meant for each other, my darling.'

'Please, Dan—let me go.' Her eyes were bright with angry tears.

'I let you go once,' he said firmly, 'but I've claimed you as my own and I'm not giving you up this time.'

'I'm not yours to claim,' she told him.

'Please listen to me, Dan—whatever you say, whatever arguments you bring to bear, it won't make any difference. I love Peter and I love my son—I won't leave them for you. I'm fond of you—but that's all. I've never loved you—I know that now.'

He pleaded with her. 'My Cathryn, why fight against Fate? God knows I've tried—I went away to free myself from my love for you but it's impossible. I went away because I doubted if we'd be happy together—now I know that our only chance of happiness is in being together.' He kissed her hair, her brow and then her lips with great tenderness. 'I'll make a devil of a husband—but we'll be happy and that's all that matters.'

With determination in her very bearing, she drew herself away from him. She walked to the hearth and replaced a fallen log with trembling hands, barely conscious of her own actions. Dan stood watching her, then he ran his hands over his dark hair and took a step towards her. Her hands moved up instinctively to ward him off.

'If you had said all this to me two years ago, my answer would have been yes,' she told him in a low voice. 'But now I'm older and wiser and I no longer love you—if love it ever was.' She sighed slightly. 'Dan, can't you see that I don't love you?'

'My instinct tells me otherwise,' he said stubbornly. 'My heart knows that you're mine. My arms ache to hold you and my love is sure of a response in you.'

She gave a helpless gesture. 'How can I convince you?' she cried. 'Dan, I won't give up my happiness with Peter—I won't give up my son.'

He snatched at her words. 'Andrew? I'm not asking that of you, my darling. He's a fine boy—I'll be proud to call him my son. I wouldn't expect you to part with him ...'

'You still don't understand! It isn't just Andrew, much as I love him. I can't—I won't—leave Peter.'

'I admire your loyalty,' he said reluctantly, 'but it's misguided, Cathryn. You never loved him. You should never have married him—but I understand why you did it. I treated you cruelly, my darling, but I'll make up for all that!'

'Is this a private conversation or can anyone join in?' asked Peter dryly from the door of the lounge.

Both Cathy and Dan swung round sharply and a quick flush rose to stain her cheeks. Dan speedily recovered his composure. 'I'm glad you've come in,' he said harshly. 'I think you should hear what I have to say and I don't want to do anything behind your back. You know that Cathryn and I love each other—you've always known it. I want her to come away with me and I'm asking you to give her her freedom so we can be married.'

'No!' Cathy cried desperately.

Peter looked from one to the other. The colour had drained from his cheeks but he walked steadily into the room and closed the door behind him.

'I admit I was afraid of this,' he said slowly.

'You must have known it would happen one day,' Dan returned. 'Now it has happened and I demand a right to our happiness.'

'Don't listen to him, Peter,' Cathy said with difficulty. 'I can't make him understand that I don't love him. Peter, I don't want to leave you!'

He sat down heavily and his face was devoid of all expression. 'If this were fifty years ago, I'd thrash the hide off you, Dan. But I suppose we must be modern and discuss the whole thing sensibly. These days, it seems to be unimportant to break up a marriage, to wrangle over a child ...' His words trailed off.

'It doesn't need much decision,' Dan declared. 'I've given you my point of view. Cathryn loves me but she's old-fashioned enough to think her first duty is to you.'

Peter threw him a cool glance. 'Well, isn't it?'

For a moment Dan was disconcerted. Then he said: 'As her husband, yes. But it would be different if I had weaned her love away from you, Peter—as it is, she's always loved me.'

'That's true,' Peter admitted. He glanced at Cathy. She sat down suddenly and buried her head in her hands. The situation seemed beyond her. Let them talk as much as they wanted, she was determined not to budge from her decision. For once in her life, she really did know herself and her emotions and nothing would induce her to give up Peter and his love for an old enchantment which had died in her. Peter was silent for a moment, wondering at her thoughts. Then he turned his frank gaze on Dan and said: 'I offered Cathy her freedom once—but I didn't know then that she was going to have a child. You would have been together long ago but for Andrew.'

Dan shrugged. 'I can't bear him a

grudge for that,' he said easily. He began to feel more confident for he knew Peter to be a fair man and one who would sacrifice his own wishes for the happiness of his wife, even if it lay in another man's arms.

'We must consider Andrew,' Peter said firmly. 'He has rights, too, Dan. The right of happiness and a family life ...'

'He'll have that,' Dan said confidently. 'He need never know that he isn't my son ...'

Peter looked at him sharply. 'You've decided his future too?'

Dan was startled by the tone of voice. But he nodded and said: 'A child needs to be with his mother—and Cathryn is devoted to him.'

'But if I refuse to let Cathy take the boy? I'm his father and surely the best person to cater for his welfare and his future?'

Dan stared at him. 'What would you want with a small boy about the place?'

Peter said and his voice was steely: 'I'm

still his father. I could get custody of him if I chose to take it to court—they aren't likely to give him to a mother who runs off with another man—the co-respondent in a divorce case.'

'You're throwing difficulties in the way,' Dan said quietly. 'I admit the truth of what you say—but I don't think you're the type of man to drag your wife through the divorce court. Naturally, you'd do the decent thing and provide Cathryn with the necessary evidence.'

'You have it all taped,' Peter said dryly. 'I'm afraid you have the advantage of knowing the way my mind works, Dan.'

Cathy looked up. 'I think you've both said enough,' she interjected. 'I've no intention of going away with Dan so all your theorizing is pretty unnecessary.'

Peter studied her face, noting the determination, the set of her chin and the hardness of her eyes. For the first time since he had loved her as a man, he was totally unconscious of her beauty. He thought only of the loyalty which was deeply ingrained in her, the sense of duty, the strong principles which she possessed—and he realized only too well that she was voluntarily rejecting the chance of happiness for his sake. His admiration and pride were stirred yet he knew that he could not allow her to do this. He turned to the man who was his friend. 'I'd like to talk to Cathy alone,' he said slowly. 'Would you mind, Dan? We can discuss this further later on.'

Dan shrugged. He was reluctant to leave them with a decision unmade yet he was shrewd enough to sense that Peter was prepared to add his persuasions so that Cathryn took the opportunity of freedom. He quickly left the room and closed the door.

For a long moment there was silence in the room. Peter took a cigarette from the box on the table and Cathy watched him light it. She wondered absently what he was going to say to her. Would he accuse her of encouraging Dan to speak?

Or would he assure her that the decision was hers alone and he did not mean to sway her either way? Whatever he said, he would not change her mind for her, she told herself firmly.

Peter was uncertain how to begin. He inhaled deeply on the cigarette and then thoughtfully blew smoke rings—a habit which intrigued and amused his small son. It reminded Cathy of Andrew and a smile flickered about her lips. As though she could ever part with him any more than she could live without Peter and know happiness. The very idea was ridiculous. She was not without sympathy for Dan but life had gone on for him during the past two years and would continue to do so in the future, no matter what he might aver in the heat of the moment.

Peter looked at Cathy and caught the last traces of the smile. Had she been thinking of Dan? He said stiffly: 'I don't want you to think that you owe me anything, Cathy. I've been very happy with you and the boy and it will be hard to lose you both. But I'm willing to agree to what you and Dan want.'

She sighed. 'Don't be so noble, Peter. Why can't you be human and fight for me with teeth and nails? Not that it's necessary because the whole suggestion came entirely from Dan and I've already told him that it's impossible.'

'Because you've got such a sense of duty,' he replied. 'If you want to go off with Dan—then do it and to hell with everyone else. It's the only way to find happiness in this world.'

She shook her head. 'That isn't true, Peter. I've proved it. I've found more happiness with you—in giving you so much—than I ever would with Dan.'

'You accused me of being noble,' he said. 'It may sound like it but my only motive is your peace of mind, Cathy. I'm grateful for everything you've done to make our marriage successful—I'm grateful for the warmth and affection you've always given me. No man could have a better wife than you ...'

'But you're quite prepared to let me go?' she chided him. She was not taking his words seriously, not even this discussion, because she had made her decision.

'I want you to go,' he replied in a low voice and she sat stunned by his words, her heart having leapt with fear and now as heavy as a stone in her breast.

'You want me to go?' she repeated incredulously.

He nodded. 'Yes.'

'Why? Why, Peter?' she demanded in a cry from her heart. Did he no longer love her? Had he waited too long for the response she now knew lived within her? Had love died for him? Was he perhaps glad of this opportunity to end their marriage? She could not believe it, for she remembered his loving caresses only the night before, the ardour of his embrace, the sweet contentment he had found in her arms—but she remembered too how silent he had been, how strangely silent for Peter, and she wondered if it had been a last farewell, if he had decided then that Dan could take her away.

Her thoughts had strangely coincided with his own if she had known it. He loved her still and his love had grown stronger and deeper during the months they had shared since their marriage. He had been patient, hoping to win her love, but with the return of Dan he had realized that his hopes were in vain and that nothing would ever erase her love for Dan. He could not go on, living with her, knowing that she still wanted Dan, so he had decided, only a moment ago, that the only way to persuade her to take the chance of happiness was to allow her to think that he no longer wanted her.

He shrugged indifferently and answered her question, construing her cry as a hopeful one, not knowing that it was moved by despair. 'What's the use of going on like this? Success or no success—our marriage was a mistake and it's time we faced facts, Cathy. The best way is divorce and Dan is right when he says that I won't drag you through the courts. Go with him, Cathy—and in time I'll supply you with the necessary evidence.'

'You really want a divorce?' she asked, shaken.

'Yes, I do.' He spoke firmly, denying the longing to catch her into his arms and plead with her to stay, to ignore his foolish words. 'The sooner the better. You can have Andrew—as Dan said, he needs a mother, and what would I do with him?'

'I can't believe this,' Cathy whispered. It seemed that her world had suddenly tumbled about her ears and she was filled with bitterness against herself that she had realized too late that the one love in her heart was for her husband.

Peter rose to his feet and tossed his cigarette into the fire. 'I'm sorry it's so unexpected,' he said curtly. 'I should have warned you before that I'd been thinking of it.'

'How—how long have you felt like this?' she stumbled through dry lips.

He shrugged. 'Does it matter?'

She nodded.

'I'm not sure,' he told her, with his back towards her. 'Perhaps it all began when we were drifting apart over Andrew—I decided to have another attempt but I guess I knew it wouldn't work.'

'I believed you were happy,' she murmured. 'You just said that you were, Peter.'

'Nevertheless, I'm not prepared to carry on,' he said stiffly. 'Dan turned up at the right moment for me ...'

'But if I don't want to go with him?' she asked.

He turned on her. 'Nonsense! Of course you do, Cathy—what's the good of pretending any more? You've always wanted him—well, here's your chance. Let's both try to find happiness elsewhere!'

CHAPTER 15

Cathy sat by Dan's side in the powerful saloon car, her eyes on the passing scenery, her face turned away from him, yet she saw nothing but a future devoid of hope, a life empty without Peter. The pain was too deep for tears. Her eyes were dark in the ashen pallor of her lovely face.

One day she might erase the memory of the last few hours but at the moment they were so vivid in her mind that she was barely conscious that Dan sat beside her, strong capable hands on the wheel, his dark eyes triumphant and a gay melody on his lips.

Peter's words had left her stunned and incredulous. Then she had risen to her feet slowly, almost falling as the pain rose to a violent crescendo which swept through her slim being. 'I understand, Peter,' she had said through stiff lips. The words had been low and tremulous but he had not turned to look at her. For a long moment she gazed at his broad, uncompromising back then she had left him, walking from the room with snatches from his remarks echoing in her ears. In a dream she had gone up to her room and thrown a few necessary things into a suitcase, hardly believing that she was about to leave her husband with his consent and blessing. She would leave Chisholm House with Dan but if he imagined that she would stay with him once they reached London, he was due for a rude awakening. She decided to go to the flat, thankful for its existence, knowing that it was at present empty and ready for her use. Travers and his wife would make her welcome and cater for her comfort—if such she could find without Peter. She knew that she could go to the Hall but she had no wish to inform her family yet that she and Peter had broken up and in her heart lingered the hope that he would change his mind.

Having packed, barely conscious exactly what possessions she had crammed into the suitcase, she returned to the lounge with her head high though her heart ached and it was an effort to stop herself trembling.

Peter and Dan were talking amicably together and it was obvious that Peter had told his friend that Cathy was prepared to leave with him. Dan agreed that they should go as soon as possible in the circumstances and he was saying this as Cathy entered. He turned to her eagerly, smiling at her with triumph and reassurance in his eyes, taking her hand and drawing her to him. Peter had watched, his expression deliberately devoid of emotion and Cathy searched his eyes in vain for some sign of emotion, regret or a last-minute indecision.

'I'm ready,' she had said numbly. She spoke to Peter without looking at him. 'Do you mind if I leave Andrew here for the time being, Peter? Until I can make some arrangements. Isobel and your mother will take good care of him.'

He nodded. 'That's all right. Naturally, you won't want to take him with you now.'

They had left soon after. Peter stood on the terrace until Dan's car began to move away then he had turned abruptly and entered the house without a backward glance. Cathy had strained to gaze at the house and the grounds until they were out of sight, her eyes hopeless and desperate, then she had sank into her seat, her hands clutched together, her whole attitude one of despair.

Dan had glanced at her. 'He took it very well,' he said and there was a touch of shame about the words. 'I hate doing this to him but it's better in the long run—he can't have been happy knowing that you've loved me all the time.' She made no reply and he turned his eyes back to the road. He was puzzled by her attitude but decided that she felt guilty about Peter and the ending of her marriage. Some minutes later, he put a tentative hand over hers and pressed them warmly. 'He'll find someone else,' he told her. 'He isn't the kind of man to live alone for the rest of his life. Don't be unhappy, darling—think of the future and how wonderful it will be to be together at last.'

'I am thinking of the future,' she had replied and he had to be content with this. He was silent after that for a long time, sensing her need to be left alone, but he could not refrain from whistling or occasionally singing a snatch of melody.

The journey seemed endless to Cathy. Now and again Dan spoke to her of trivial things and she made a reply but she was disinclined for conversation and made no effort to speak to him.

They were nearing London now and relief flooded Cathy but she yet had to convince Dan that leaving Peter did not mean that she meant to marry him or that she still loved him.

Now he turned to her and said blithely: 'We'll go abroad, darling—wherever you like. I don't want to take you to Norfolk until we're married—it would be unpleasant for you and people will talk enough about the divorce, anyway, without giving them food for gossip at this stage. Where would you go, my Cathryn—France, Spain, America? All of them? We'll do whatever you say.' Confidence rang in his voice and she moved restlessly, raising a hand to brush back a few strands of hair from her brow.

'You and I aren't going anywhere, Dan,' she said decisively.

He threw her an amazed glance. 'What do you mean?'

'Isn't it obvious? I've no intention of making my life with you—as I've already tried to impress on you, I don't love you and I've no wish to marry you.'

His whole attitude was one of disbelief.

'But—you've left Peter—he told me that he'd persuaded you to take your happiness, not to consider him ...'

'I don't care what Peter told you—it isn't true. No one persuaded me.'

'Then why—?' He broke off and then muttered an oath under his breath. 'I don't understand all this, Cathryn—why are you with me now if you don't love me, if we aren't going to be married?'

'I'm only with you now because you have a car and I want to go to London,' she told him coldly. 'You know the address of the flat—I shall be very grateful if you'll drop me off there.'

He slammed on the brakes and stopped the car. The road was a little-used one and very little traffic was in sight. 'That's very cool!' he said slowly, anger rising in him. 'I can't believe that you know what you're saying.'

'Of course I do. The real truth is that you can't believe that I prefer Peter to you but I do—you imagined that I'd jump at the chance of going off with you in search of happiness. Search? It would be a long search indeed and I doubt if I'd ever find it.' She glanced at his stricken face. 'I'm sorry, Dan,' she added more kindly. 'I know that you do care for me but it's impossible—I shouldn't have used you like this. I shouldn't have misled you, my dear. I left Buckhurst today because I want to get away for a while, to have time to think—not because I loved you and wanted to break up my marriage.'

He said oddly: 'Peter thinks the same as I do—have you deliberately misled him?'

She shook her head. 'No. He thinks that I'm going with you wherever you choose to take me.'

He seized her hands and carried them to his lips, one after the other, kissing the fingers with tender passion. 'My Cathryn, you're unhappy and confused—I understand how you feel. You want time to think—and you shall have it. I'll take you to the flat if that's what you want.'

He smiled reassuringly into her eyes. 'I've rushed you off your feet, darling,' he said ruefully. 'There's never been time to court you properly—now I will. You shall have everything your way and I know that in time you'll be sure of your love for me and will want to marry me as much as I want you for my wife.' He bent his head and brushed her lips gently with his warm, eager mouth. 'I love you,' he murmured. 'Remember that—and think of the happiness we can share.'

She gave up the hopeless task of convincing him for the time being. Eventually he would be forced to see that she was sincere and determined in what she told him. Let him cling to his dreams for a little while—they would all be smashed when realization reached him and she knew only too well the pain that could accompany the shattering of dreams.

He drove on and now he talked soothingly and well to her, attempting to smooth away the doubts and fears and impress upon her what a gentle and considerate lover he would prove to be, that things should be just as she wanted, not only now but always, assuring her that he would be patient for he had the confidence of eventual victory. She let him talk but she scarcely listened and she knew that none of his arguments or pleas would bear fruit in her mind. There was no trace of the love—the wild, sweet enchantment—which she had once felt for him. Only pain was present in her heart and thoughts, even blotting out her love for Peter and Andrew until the pain had lessened a little.

He drove to the flat but she would not let him come up with her. After a few moments of trying to persuade her, he gave in reluctantly. He slid an arm about her shoulders and drew her towards him but she resisted him, her hand on his chest.

'No, Dan,' she said firmly.

His dark brows lowered. 'Don't be difficult, darling.'

'Oh, for goodness sake!' she snapped, losing her patience. 'Why can't you understand, Dan? I don't want you now or ever—why won't you face facts?'

'Because I won't believe that you mean it,' he countered. 'I promised to be patient and I will be, my Cathryn—but don't make me wait too long.' He leaned across and opened the door. 'Run away then, if you must—but tonight we'll go to the theatre or a night club, whatever you want. I'll call for you at eight.'

She shook her head. 'I'm not going out tonight. I want to be alone, Dan. I told you, I want time to think—and that means being by myself.'

He gestured helplessly. 'As you please. But I'll telephone you.'

She breathed a heartfelt sigh of relief when she reached the flat. She fumbled in her handbag for the key and then realized that she had left it at Buckhurst. So she rang the bell and a moment later the door was opened by Travers. He looked surprised to see her, but stood back for her to enter.

'I'm sorry—there wasn't time to ring you,' she said wearily. 'Are any of the family staying here?'

'No, Miss Cathy.' He took the coat as she slipped it from her shoulders. She threw her bag and gloves on a nearby table and indicated her case.

'Take that into my room, would you, Travers? And ask Mrs Travers to make me a pot of tea. I don't want anything to eat.'

'Will you be staying in Town long?' he asked.

She shrugged. 'I'm not sure. A few weeks, possibly.'

'Very good, Miss Cathy.' He left the room with her suitcase and she threw herself into an armchair and rested her head on one hand, closing her eyes. The events of the day coupled with the journey had utterly wearied her and her brain was reeling with a rush of thoughts.

Why? If only she knew the answer. Why had her marriage broken up in this way? Why did Peter no longer want to go on—had his patience finally given out just when it had been rewarded by her new knowledge that she loved him? Why was he willing—indeed, anxious—for her to go away with Dan? Why would he not believe that she wanted nothing but a future with him? So many questions stirred to break through the numb despair. What was she going to do now? Peter did not want her—and she did not want Dan. She could not stay indefinitely here at the flat and she shrank from going back to Buckhurst, kind and affectionate though her family would always be, understanding though they would prove to be at this turning-point in her life. The Hall was too near Chisholm House and she would see Peter too often, be reminded too much of all she had lost and wanted so very much to regain. She had never before regretted the closeness of their two homes or the friendly intimacy between the two families but now it was painful to her to remember it.

She was very lonely and dispirited during the next few days but she would not give in to Dan's repeated requests for her company, ignoring all his appeals and merely repeating what she had already told him until she tired of the repetition. He telephoned her two or three times a day, called at the flat daily, sent her flowers and gifts and was no doubt going about his wooing of her in the manner which had always won him what he wanted in the past. But it was useless where Cathy was concerned for her determination was firm and immovable.

'Dan, please go back to Norfolk and leave me alone,' she pleaded with him one day. 'No matter what you say, my mind is made up and nothing will change it.'

He threw his cigarette into the hearth with an impatient gesture. 'Then what do you intend to do?' he demanded angrily.

'I don't know.' She sighed. 'I hope one day to go back to Peter and make every effort to save our marriage.'

'Then you admit it's on the rocks?' he caught her up sharply.

She had never told him what Peter had said to her for she was too proud to admit that she loved a man who no longer wanted her despite the happiness they had known together. Now she replied evenly: 'No, I don't. I think that we simply need a few weeks apart.'

'But you spoke of taking Andrew away—that seems to me as though you're considering divorce or separation at least.'

'Who knows what the future holds?' she retorted. 'I only know mine isn't with you, Dan, and never will be.'

'You loved me once,' he reminded her. 'I know that very well and I won't believe any denial. In your heart, you know that you love me still—I can't understand you, Cathryn. If you and Peter are washed up—and it certainly looks like it—then why not marry me? I'll make you happy. I swear it!'

She shook her head. 'I know you'd do your best, Dan. I'm sorry that you love me so much and I never wanted to hurt you—please believe me!' She caught his arm. 'I love Peter as much as you love me—you must be able to understand and sympathize. Help me, Dan—please go away and leave me to work things out on my own. Can't you see that you confuse and disturb me—how can I think straight if I have to keep fighting against your persuasions?'

'Then it is a fight?' he asked quickly. 'You really know that I'm right—you want to say yes but your ridiculous sense of duty or convention or whatever it is stops you from being happy with me? Is that it? I don't give a hang for duty or convention ...!'

'That's why you're not the man to make me a good husband,' she retorted. 'Dan, you and I are totally different people. We wouldn't be happy together—we're too unsuited to each other. I can see that even if you can't. You're in love with your conception of me—not the person I really am.'

He looked at her obliquely through long thick lashes. 'So that's the way you worked it out for yourself, my Cathryn, is it? You assured yourself that you were in love with a dream—that you hadn't seen me enough or known me well enough to love the man I am? Now I begin to see daylight.' He moved quickly and took her into his arms. 'My poor darling—you're not only fighting me, you're fighting your love for me which I know is very real and wonderful ...'

She struggled in his arms, thankful that his closeness no longer had any power over her, thankful that her heart did not leap or her blood surge in her veins. It was further proof that no trace of her love lingered and she was glad that she had not been mistaken.

The door opened behind them and

Diana said: 'Why, Cathy? What are you doing here?'

Dan released her immediately and swung round. The colour surged into Cathy's cheeks at the sight of her younger half-sister who had so unexpectedly entered. She still held the doorkey in her hand and it was obvious from her startled face that she had expected to find an empty flat for Cathy had kept her whereabouts a secret from her family. She had telephoned Peter and asked him to tell them that she was visiting friends and told him that in time she would explain things to them herself. It had been apparent from his coldness on the telephone that he believed her to be with Dan and he had cut the conversation very short, much to her dismay.

Diana sauntered into the room, a smile beginning to touch her lips. 'A clandestine meeting?' she asked lightly. She stretched out a hand. 'It's Dan Ritchie, isn't it?

Quite a long time since I saw you—but I've read about you in the papers. How are you?'

Dan had quickly recovered his composure. He took her hand and held it warmly for a moment, admiring the attractive picture Diana made in the soft green tweed, her short dark hair windblown and her cheeks rosy from the cold. He was surprised to find her so adult and poised but reminded himself that it was over two years since he had seen her and girls grew up very quickly.

'You're Diana, of course,' he replied. 'You were barely more than a child when we last met.'

She threw him a provocative glance. 'How like a man to remind me of that?' She turned to Cathy. 'I'm quite sophisticated these days, aren't I, Cathy? But what are you doing here? I had no idea you were using the flat.'

Dan said: 'I must be going. I'll call you

later, Cathryn.' He gave Diana a warm, vibrant smile. 'Perhaps we'll see each other again soon?'

She laughed. 'In another two years' time, I expect—or has the wanderer returned for good?'

Dan shrugged. 'Who knows?'

When the two girls were alone, Cathy picked up a cigarette box and offered it to Diana. She took one and then said: 'Darling, tell me if I'm interfering, but does Peter know that Dan's back in circulation?'

Cathy glanced at her quickly, wondering how much the girl had known of her mad infatuation for Dan in the past. 'Of course he does,' she replied automatically, 'but I doubt if he's very much concerned. I've left him.'

Diana stared at her. 'You've left Peter?' She was horrified. But then she caught her breath and added: 'That explains a lot of things—Cathy, how could you? Peter worships the ground you walk on ... How could you leave him for a man like Dan Ritchie?'

Cathy sighed. 'I haven't. Dan doesn't mean a thing to me.'

'But he was kissing you when I came in,' Diana said dryly.

'He was not!' Cathy retorted sharply.

Diana exhaled blue-grey cigarette smoke and her eyes were disbelieving. 'I see. He was merely offering you comfort in the only way he knows.'

'You hardly know Dan,' Cathy reminded her.

She laughed. 'Perhaps not. But I've heard a lot. That's the trouble with these handsome men with a reputation—it always follows them about. Anyway, we're not discussing Dan Ritchie. I'm interested in what you've just told me. Peter hasn't breathed a word—he told us you were visiting friends.' She frowned. 'I thought he was rather vague and disinclined to talk about your sudden departure.'

'How is he?' Cathy asked eagerly. 'Is he

well—does he seem depressed? Oh, Diana, do you think he misses me?' Suddenly she put her face in her hands and began to sob bitterly, her whole body shaking. It was the first time that tears had come to relieve the dull pain which lived with her.

CHAPTER 16

Peter sat with clenched hands between his knees. Diana roamed restlessly about the room, smoking a cigarette, her dark hair dishevelled. She talked quickly and with emphasis and he listened in silence.

At last he looked up. 'Why didn't she tell me she was here?' he demanded.

She gave a helpless gesture with her hands.

'You told me the answer to that yourself, Peter. Didn't you tell her that you didn't want her any longer, that you welcomed the chance to end your marriage, that she should go away with Dan Ritchie and give you both a chance to be happy with someone else? Can't you imagine what must have gone through her mind, Peter? She loves you and she thought you loved her. It was the only security she had—or so she thought—and suddenly it was swept away from her. Of course she wasn't going to tell you that she was living here alone and desperately unhappy. No more would I—nor would any woman in the circumstances.'

He rose to his feet and walked to the window. 'Why doesn't she come in? She's been out for hours—why didn't she tell you where she was going?'

'I didn't want her to know you were coming,' she reminded him. 'I told her that I was having a man friend to lunch and so she's tactfully vanished for the afternoon. She'll be back soon, don't worry.'

He turned quickly. 'I want to see her, Diana—you can't imagine what it's been like without her, imagining her with Dan, thinking—oh my God, all sorts of things ...' His voice broke and trailed off.

Diana put her hand on his arm. 'I know, Peter. You're both a pair of idiots and I'd like to knock your heads together.'

She paused and added diffidently: 'You don't think I've been interfering—ringing you and telling you that Cathy was here and needed you?'

He smiled down at her, laying his hand on hers and pressing it warmly. 'Of course you're an interfering little hussy—and thank goodness for it! Cathy and I could have gone on like this for months—with me thinking she was somewhere abroad with Dan and hesitating to provide her with the evidence I promised and yet knowing that I dare not let her down—and Cathy thinking that I no longer loved her ...' He broke off and searched her face eagerly. 'You're sure she loves me, Diana? She did say that?'

She nodded. 'Many times and I know she means it. Of course she loves you—all your lives you two have been meant for each other—I can't see how she ever gave Dan a second thought when you were always around.'

'Possibly that was the trouble,' he said ruefully. 'I was always around—and Cathy just thought of me as faithful old Pete, a standby in trouble and a willing salve to her pride when Dan walked out on her.'

'Well, if that's true, she doesn't think of you like that now,' Diana said firmly. 'She'll never be happy without you—besides, Peter, you're too well-suited to split up. I've never known a better matched couple.'

'We nearly split up over Andrew,' he reminded her.

'That was different,' she said firmly. 'Besides, you would have sorted things out eventually.' She laughed. 'But I'm too impatient—I like to do a bit of interfering now and again. I think it's so silly to waste time with unhappiness and misunderstanding when you love someone—life is so short, anyway.' She tapped his arm sharply. 'As for you, Peter Wallis—if you ever try being noble again, I shall definitely lose my temper with you.'

'I can't risk that,' he said and he smiled but he was edgy and ill-at-ease, longing to see Cathy, wondering where the devil she was and hoping with all his heart that Diana had not misconstrued her words and that Cathy really did love him. He had been thoroughly miserable without her, regretting every moment of the day that he had sent her away when he needed her so much, spending as much time as he could with his small son because he was a reminder of Cathy and eased the pain a little with his childish chatter and at the same time glad of the pain it brought when the boy asked again and again for 'Mummy'.

Cathy dragged herself into the block wearily. She had whiled away the long hours by doing a little shopping, dropping in to a cinema and then having a solitary tea at Fullers. Idly, she wondered about Diana's friend and hoped he had gone by now for she was in no mood for socialities. She dreaded the thought of spending another evening by herself in the flat for Diana was enjoying her few days in

Town and could not be expected to forfeit her entertainment to spend her time with her sister. Cathy had no heart to go out although she had many friends in Town who would be glad to see her. She had gone with Bess to the theatre one evening, merely explaining that she was up on a shopping spree. Bess, thoughtless and frivolous as ever, accepted the explanation without question and gladly accompanied Cathy to the theatre on the one evening when she was free from other engagements. She was loving every day that she lived in Town, sharing a flat with a girlfriend, surrounded by many admirers who willingly escorted her to night clubs, theatres and parties which were necessary to life, in Bess' opinion.

Cathy opened the door with the spare key that Travers had provided and went directly to her room to take off her outdoor clothes and tidy her hair. It was a tactful thought for she knew that Diana would have heard her come in and would want a few minutes grace to prepare her friend for the introduction—unless he had already left. She wondered if Diana were still in but it was only a passing thought.

She studied herself in the mirror of her dressing-table and put up her hand to rub some colour into her pale cheeks. She wore the strain of fatigue for she was not sleeping well and pain had left its trace in her green eyes. Carelessly, she powdered her nose and applied fresh lipstick. Taking a brush, she ran it through her hair and then rose languidly from the stool. Crossing to the window, she looked down on the square below in its stark coat of winter and she longed for the summer to come, hoping that the sunshine and warmth would raise her spirits a little, hoping that by then she would have learned to bear her pain bravely and accept life more philosophically.

Diana heard her come in and turned to Peter eagerly. 'There she is. I'm going out now, Peter.' She glanced at her watch. 'I shall only be a few minutes late for my appointment, after all. I'm leaving you to it—and don't spoil things this time, there's a good lad!' She strained up on her toes to kiss his cheek warmly and with sincere affection. She was a tall woman and she did not have far to stretch. 'I've done what I could,' she added. 'Now it's up to you!'

Peter took a fresh cigarette and then stubbed it as soon as it was alight. He sat down, tapping his fingers restlessly on the arm of the chair, and then he stood up again and wandered about the room. He stood by the bookshelves, scanning them with unseeing eyes.

How long Cathy was taking! Perhaps it had not been Cathy, after all! How would she react when she saw him? Would she know that Diana had sent for him? Would she resent his unexpected presence at the flat? Was it true that she had been unhappy without him, that she loved him, that she did not want Dan? Why had she not gone with Dan after all? Or had she—and then changed her mind about him? He was tortured by doubts and questions, hopes and fears.

He ran his hands through his hair and then looked at those same hands, trembling now with excitement and nerves. His stomach muscles were taut and his collar was tight about his neck. He put up a hand to ease the neckband of his white shirt and then hastily straightened his tie which he had pushed awry.

He turned away from the bookshelves and looked around the room—large, expensively and comfortably furnished, pleasant and charming, cool in summer and heated centrally in winter. It was in this very room that Cathy had first told him that she was going to have Andrew: it was in this room that Dan had sat with them before he left London for Norfolk prior to his departure for America—how long ago that seemed now. Peter remembered the glances which had passed between Dan and Cathy and

337

the tension he had sensed at the time. He had known the love which flowed between them and read into Dan's parting words the farewell which she too had understood and accepted. Was it really possible that her love was no more—that she had turned from Dan to him in all sincerity? Or was the truth that she could not bring herself to defy convention—to bring divorce into their families—to spark off the round of gossip which would affect them all? He did not know the answer but he clung to Diana's reputation for honesty and knew that she had only spoken what she believed to be true. But she might have been mistaken. Or Cathy might be prepared to return to him for his sake, to save his happiness, willing to give up Dan so that her husband should not suffer unnecessarily—in fact, being as noble as Peter himself had been for her sake, allowing her to think that his love was dead when it was so much a part of him that he would never be free of it and never wanted to be.

Cathy came into the room wearing the guarded, social expression necessary for meeting her sister's friend. Her eyes widened at sight of Peter standing alone, his fair hair rumpled and his very body turned towards her with eager anticipation in every line. She glanced about for Diana, puzzled.

Peter had hoped vaguely that Cathy might run into his arms or at least give some sign of her joy at seeing him again. But he was disappointed. She stood for a long moment with her hand still on the door then she slowly closed it behind her and came further into the room.

'Why did you come here?' she asked in a cool voice, striving to hide the emotion which welled in her.

'You don't sound very pleased to see me,' he replied ruefully.

'How did you know I was here ... oh, of course—Diana!' she exclaimed with a wealth of discovery in her tone. She instantly regretted that she had confided in the girl but it had been done on impulse and she was dismayed to find that Diana had betrayed her confidence.

Peter nodded. 'Yes, I have Diana to thank.' He moved towards her and her heart leaped but he merely drew out his cigarette case and offered it to her politely. He was very nervous and afraid of saying or doing the wrong thing. If he had followed his heart, she would be in his arms by now but he did not want to antagonize her with over-confidence. She shook her head to his offer and a bitter humour twisted her lips into a smile.

'You know I don't smoke,' she reminded him. She picked up a table-lighter and flicked it into life. He bent his head over the flame and she was moved by the impulse to put up a hand to smooth the ruffled hair. But she fought down the impulse, turning to replace the lighter on the low table by her side. 'How is Andrew?' she asked him evenly.

'He's fine—but he misses you, Cathy,' he told her.

Her eyes clouded suddenly. 'I expect he does. I've never left him before—his little world must be all upside down, poor darling.' She looked up at Peter squarely. 'I'm afraid I haven't made any arrangements for him yet—it doesn't seem fair to coop him up in a flat and it's difficult to find nannies in London. Isobel won't want to leave Buckhurst if she's still going to marry Hinckley in the spring ...'

'Cathy—why take Andrew away from the home and surroundings he's always known?' He caught her hand. 'I'm not doing this very well—I hoped you might know why I came and help me a little. Cathy—you're not with Dan? If you've changed your mind about him, then come back with me now to Buckhurst. Let's try again—I've missed you so much, my dear.' His voice rang with sincerity and his blue eyes were rich with appeal.

She raised her head sharply, sudden life

springing to her eyes. She searched his face eagerly, noting the warmth in his expression, the tentative curve to his lips, sensing his inner soberness. Did he really want her back? Had he found it impossible to be happy without her? Had he been miserable since she left Chisholm House? Hopefully, she sought some sign in his fair, beloved face. If she went back to him, would he always believe that she loved Dan in reality but was prepared to accept second-best and find a lesser happiness? Would she ever be able to convince him that she had never loved Dan as a woman but as an enchanted child? Could she find the ways to show him that she loved him with all her heart?

'Do you know why I'm not with Dan?' she asked slowly.

He shrugged a little impatiently. 'Diana ...' he began and then broke off abruptly. How could he tell her that Diana had assured him that his wife really loved and wanted him? Such assurance could only come from the lips and arms of Cathy herself and he did not want to force words from her which were not from her heart.

'Still being noble, Peter?' she asked, raising her chin proudly though the ache in her heart struck anew. 'I'm beginning to understand now. Diana told you that I was unhappy without you, that I regretted leaving Buckhurst, that I'd realized how silly I've always been to care about Dan when I've had you by my side all the time, that I know now that I love you—all the things I told her. So you're prepared to forget everything and take me back as though it had never happened.' She threw a taunt at him: 'You always did enjoy playing the martyr, Peter.'

He ignored the sneer. 'All these things you told Diana—were they true, Cathy? Have you been unhappy? Do you regret leaving me?' He paused and looked searchingly into her eyes. 'These would be enough for me to welcome you back with open arms—but if the last is also true, then I know that all the years of waiting have been worthwhile.' He raised her hands to his lips. 'Do you really love me, Cathy?' he asked gently.

'Will you believe me if I say that I do?' she countered sadly. She released her fingers from his hold and turned away from him. 'I've pretended to you so often that I loved you so that you would be happy, Peter—I thought I deceived you but now I know that you've always known the truth. I was crazy about Dan—and crazy is the operative word. There was no sense in my love for him—and I wouldn't even call it love now. Infatuation, enchantment—I don't know. Whatever it was, it's ended now.' She spread her hands in a gesture of finality. 'Will you understand if I say that my only emotion now is a great need of you, Peter—an aching need, a desperate need, a sense of belonging to you and wanting you, a crying out against the end of our marriage.'

'I understand,' he murmured huskily.

'I understand because that's the way I feel, Cathy, darling—I've always felt that where you're concerned. All my life I've known that we belonged together—but if you thought your happiness lay elsewhere then I could not keep you tied to me.'

Suddenly she turned to him and his arms were about her, drawing her close. She knew the comforting familiarity of his presence and her heart was light because she knew that he would always be there when she wanted him, his arms would always be open for her to run into, and he offered her a great and peaceful security, a loyalty and a love which had never seemed so precious until she had nearly thrown it away.

'Hold me close,' she begged. 'Hold me, darling—never let me go.'

His arms tightened about her and she drew on his strength and the love which flowed from him—a love which could be expressed for the first time in full without fear or rebuff or disappointment. His lips touched her hair as he replied softly: 'I'll never let you go, dearest—you're safe with me.'

She began to cry and the salt tears were a healing balm for the pain she had known. She wept noiselessly and the tears ran down her cheeks unchecked. At last, he lifted her chin and fumbled for his handkerchief to wipe away the drops of sorrow and bitter regret. He smiled at her.

'This is a wet reunion, I must say,' he teased and was glad that a smile broke through the storm, lighting her face with sunshine.

'I'm sorry,' she said quickly. 'I'm being silly—but I've missed you so much and I thought I'd never be happy again!'

She sounded so dramatic that he had to repress the laugh which bubbled within him for he would not hurt her for the world by making light of all she had suffered. He lightly kissed her now. 'I love you,' he whispered. 'I love you more than anything else in the world—no man ever loved as I love you.'

She clung to him again and this time she lifted her face for his kiss. Their lips met and held and she knew the familiar eager warmth, the gentle and loving tenderness of his kiss. When he raised his head, she caught his face between her hands and her eyes were adoring. 'I love you, Peter—so very much.'

There was no doubting her declaration now. Her eyes blazed with truth and her voice vibrated with warm sincerity. 'Can you forget that I once put Dan Ritchie before you, darling? Will you forgive? Will you give me the chance to prove my love in every way I know?'

He kissed her again. 'I don't think I could ever have given you up really, Cathy—I hoped you would tire of Dan when you'd lived with him a while. I certainly didn't intend to give you evidence for a divorce for a long time and nothing would induce me to drag you through the courts. You aren't the sort of person to be happy living with a man who wasn't your husband—and I believed you would one day want to come back to me. I was prepared to wait for that day—thank goodness it came quicker than I dared hope—and thank Diana for making it possible!'

She released herself from his arms.

'Darling, post-mortems later. Now I must get my things together. I'm not staying in London another day—with or without you—and it will be a long time before I voluntarily come to Town again. I'm longing to see Andrew and hold him in my arms—I could never have given him up, you know. If you had refused to let me have him, then I would have come back if only for Andrew's sake!'

He teased her: 'Are you sure that's not your reason for coming back now?'

She threw him a reproachful glance. Then she laughed. 'I can see that I didn't make myself quite clear just now,' she said lightly and she stood very close to him, deliberately provocative, stirring his senses. She put her arms about his neck and pressed her mouth ardently against his, expressing all her real and deep love in the kiss she gave him. His arms drew her closer against him straining her slim young body against his hard chest with rising passion. When she drew away, she laughed into his blue eyes. 'Well, have you any doubts now?' she teased him and he shook his head.

'None at all,' she sighed happily and his smile tugged at her heart. How had she been so blind for such a long time to the love that filled her entire being? But there was no need now for questions and doubts—they belonged in the past with the spectre of Dan Ritchie who would never again have the power to stir her heart. She had escaped from the enchanted castle in the midst of young dreams—and she was finding that reality was far more wonderful and worthwhile.

This Large Print Book for the Partially sighted, who cannot read normal print, is published under the auspices of

THE ULVERSCROFT FOUNDATION